PRAISE FOR

A Holiday Miracle in Apple Blossom

"If you're looking for a sweet, old-fashioned Christmas story, this is it!"

REBECCA JAMISON, author of
Persuasion: A Latter-day Tale and *Emma: A Latter-day Tale*

"The debut novella from author June McCrary Jacobs will break your heart for little Mary Noel and the tragedy she has to deal with. Then your heart will rejoice as the town comes together to help her and her family in their time of need. A sweet story for your Christmas story collection."

CINDY C BENNETT, author of *Rapunzel Untangled*

"A moving story of love and encouragement. Filled with memorable characters that will touch your heart, June Jacob's A Holiday Miracle in Apple Blossom should be at the top of everyone's holiday reading list."

MANDI TUCKER SLACK, author
of *The Alias* and *Tide Ever Rising*

"What happens when you put others first? Paul and Amber find out while uniting a town to bring a Christmas miracle to a little girl. So snuggle under a beloved quilt, grab a cup of hot cocoa, and enjoy a few hours of sweet holiday reading that will leave you wanting to serve someone too."

T. LYNN ADAMS, author of the Tomb of Terror series

A HOLIDAY MIRACLE IN *Apple Blossom*

A NOVEL

JUNE MCCRARY JACOBS

SWEETWATER BOOKS
AN IMPRINT OF CEDAR FORT, INC.
SPRINGVILLE, UTAH

This is a work of fiction. The characters, names, incidents, places, and dialogue are products of the author's imagination and are not to be construed as real.

ISBN 13: 978-1-4621-1352-1

Published by Sweetwater Books, an imprint of Cedar Fort, Inc.
2373 W. 700 S., Springville, UT 84663
Distributed by Cedar Fort, Inc., www.cedarfort.com

LIBRARY OF CONGRESS CATALOGING-IN-PUBLICATION DATA

Jacobs, June McCrary.
  A holiday miracle in Apple Blossom / June McCrary Jacobs.
     pages cm
   ISBN 978-1-4621-1352-1 (hardback with dust jacket : alk. paper)
  1. Post-traumatic stress disorder in children--Fiction. 2. Psychological fiction. I. Title.
  PS3610.A356435H65 2013
  813'.6--dc23
                         2013017821

Cover design by Angela D. Olsen
Additional design by Kelsey Webb and Rebecca J. Greenwood
Cover design © 2013 by Lyle Mortimer
Edited and typeset by Melissa Caldwell

Printed in the United States of America

10 9 8 7 6 5 4 3 2 1

*This book is dedicated to my exceptional husband,
in honor of our thirtieth wedding anniversary.
Thank you for always listening to me whenever
I said, "Let's make up a story about this."
You're the best . . .*

CHAPTER ONE

Humming her favorite patriotic tune as she worked, Amber Kellen was startled when the sharp click of the heels of her principal, Dorothy Griffin, echoed loudly on the linoleum floor of her classroom. Amber stopped pinning the brightly hued autumn landscapes painted by her six-year-old students on the front bulletin board in her classroom and turned to greet Mrs. Griffin. The affable and capable leader of the staff and students of Apple Blossom Country School wore a tense expression that caused her normally relaxed face to appear pale and drawn.

The young first-grade teacher gasped as the realization that something must be seriously amiss gripped her heart. As the principal approached, Mrs. Griffin knit her eyebrows together and shook her head sadly. Amber had noticed that the school administrator always spoke formally no matter what the situation. It was likely as a result of her university degree in Shakespearean literature.

"Amber, I regret having to greet you with such horrific news this Monday morning. Especially since we're returning from our Thanksgiving weekend break."

"What's happened?" Amber heard a slight tremor in her voice.

"One of your students was critically injured in a tragic accident yesterday afternoon."

Her open palm flying to cover her heart, Amber squeaked, "Who? What happened?"

"Mary Noel Simmons was hit by a car on the road in front of her house."

"Oh, no," Amber shivered involuntarily.

"As you can imagine, the driver of the vehicle is absolutely distraught over what occurred. The police investigation found that the driver hit the little girl and her dog through no fault of his own. It was plain and simply a freak accident." The middle-aged administrator paused briefly. "Apparently the dog's leash got tangled around the bicycle's handlebars. When the dog took off across the road to chase a cat, Mary Noel got dragged out into the street too. The pair darted out from behind a big travel trailer that was parked in front of a neighbor's property. What a shock for everyone involved."

"Oh, this is terrible! I'm almost afraid to ask—how is Mary Noel?"

"Her parents say it could have been a lot worse. As it is, Mary Noel has a compound fracture in her left leg and a broken wrist that will require several surgeries. She has a lot of cuts and bruises along with a mild concussion. Fortunately, Mary Noel avoided a severe concussion or more serious permanent complications because she was wearing her helmet." Mrs. Griffin fidgeted with her hands and sighed deeply. Amber prepared herself for the worst because it was obvious that the administrator had more bad news to share. "According to Mary Noel's mother, Barbara Simmons, those aren't the worst injuries, I'm afraid."

Silence filled the classroom as both women processed the profound ramifications of the accident. "Please tell me everything," Amber said. "I'd rather hear it from you now than let my imagination run wild." She physically braced herself against her sturdy, wooden teacher's desk for support.

"As you wish. Mary Noel was traumatized by the sight of her little dog, Cocoa, dying in the accident. By all accounts, the two were inseparable. Since Mary Noel didn't lose consciousness, she saw and heard everything. Even though the dog died almost instantly, there was a copious amount of blood and—well, you get the picture."

Amber detected some tender emotions surfacing

in her principal's usual stalwart manner. Mrs. Griffin's voice was shaky as she continued, "Mary Noel has completely withdrawn into herself since the accident. That little girl hasn't muttered a single word, not even to her mom, dad, or grandparents. Barbara Simmons told me the doctor's opinion is that it's *not* Mary Noel's injuries that have caused the youngster to withdraw. No, the physician firmly believes it was seeing her best friend, Cocoa, killed that has shocked this little girl into silence."

Nodding her head in understanding, Amber responded, "Mary Noel frequently talked about her little Scottie dog, Cocoa. Apparently the two were the very best of friends and constant companions. I can't imagine how sad and lonesome Mary Noel must be feeling right now."

"Yes, well, that sadness along with her physical injuries will ensure that little Mary Noel will miss much of this semester of school. She'll likely not return to class until after Christmas vacation, if then."

"This is so upsetting. Do the Simmonses want the other kids in my class to know what happened, or should I keep this to myself?"

"You are exceptionally perceptive for being so young and inexperienced in the classroom." Mrs. Griffin smiled gently. "The Simmonses felt you could let your class know that she's in the hospital without including all of the gory details about poor Cocoa.

Mrs. Simmons thought your students could make Mary Noel some cute cards and paint some pictures that the family can use to decorate the hospital room. The doctors won't release the girl from the hospital until her mental condition improves greatly. Who knows? Maybe some cheery cards from her class-mates will do the trick."

"I think Mrs. Simmons's idea is a good one. The class and I will work on some greeting cards and pictures today. I'll deliver them to the family at the hospital on my way home this afternoon. Is there anything else I can do?"

"I tend to think the less said about the extent of Mary Noel's injuries and the dog's death the better. We need to focus on being positive and send Mary Noel our love and good wishes at this time. Perhaps you can just tell the other children that Mary Noel isn't feeling well, and she needs their friendship to cheer up."

"I totally agree. I need to spend some time reflecting on what's happened. It's the only way I can deal with this type of stress; I need to gather my thoughts before school begins. I want to be composed and calm when I announce the situation to the children."

Mrs. Griffin added, "Let me know if you need anything at all, Amber. With the Lord's grace, we'll all get through this together somehow or another."

Amber felt comforted by her administrator's gentle pat on her own trembling hand.

"Thanks for your support. I really appreciate your telling me about this in person rather than letting me hear about it in the staff room at recess."

"You're very welcome. I'll make a brief announcement to the other teachers and staff members so that you won't have to shoulder the responsibility for being the public information officer for the school. Do everything in your power to have a good day with your students. I'll keep you posted on Mary Noel's condition when I hear anything at all."

"I'd appreciate that, Mrs. Griffin. Have a good day."

❊ ❊ ❊

Alone once again, Amber paced the floor while processing the devastating news her principal had shared with her. As she glanced out the window at the playground beyond, Amber paused to appreciate the extraordinary earthy hues of autumn's golden browns, burnt oranges, and vivid yellows in the abundance of maple, beech, birch, elm, and ash leaves suspended precariously from the half empty trees surrounding the property. Apple Blossom, Vermont, certainly was a picturesque setting in autumn.

Bowing her head, Amber became still as she prayed. "Father, please be with Mary Noel in her time of need. Bless Mary Noel's doctors and parents as they try to choose the best course of action to aid in healing her injuries and other hurts. Thank you. Amen."

As a familiar peace and comfort washed over her soul, she noted the time on the old-fashioned clock hanging behind her desk. She had exactly thirty minutes before her students would begin trooping in to begin another day of learning and growth. Amber neatly printed a list of vocabulary words on the whiteboard for her students to use when making their cards and letters for Mary Noel. She included "Mary Noel, cheer, better, hope, soon, friend, sincerely" and several other words she felt would convey the classmates' message to the traumatized little girl.

Amber smiled as she recalled Mary Noel's sparkling blue eyes and whimsical expression when she'd recently shared with her classmates about the antics of her beloved Scottish terrier, Cocoa. Since the first day of school, Mary Noel had repeatedly asked Amber if she could bring her pet to school for show and tell. Amber had gently declined each time, rationalizing that she didn't want her classroom to turn into a circus with pets trooping in every Friday afternoon.

Now Amber was feeling quite selfish and even somewhat guilty for her unwillingness to allow the little Scottie dog to visit her classroom. "I hope Mary

Noel will forgive me," Amber murmured aloud wistfully.

❄ ❄ ❄

Amber's students began arriving a few minutes before the official start of school. Their somber looks told her that they had most likely already heard the sad news about Mary Noel's accident. More than one child stopped by Amber's desk for a comforting hug before moving to their assigned seats. By the time all of the desks, save one, were filled, silence thickened the air with tension and sorrow.

"Good morning, boys and girls." Amber felt she failed miserably when she tried to share her usual welcoming smile with the children.

"Miss Kellen, I'm very sad today," blurted out Mary Noel's best friend, Janae Montanez. Lower lip trembling, Janae poured out her feelings to her teacher and classmates, "My best friend, Mary Noel, is living at the hospital. She got hitted by a car yesterday." A torrent of tears began to flow from Janae's dark brown eyes. Overcome with emotion, the girl lay her head down on her desk and sobbed.

"I heard about the accident from Mrs. Griffin this morning, boys and girls. It made me very sad to think that Mary Noel is hurt and in so much pain," the teacher said.

"Yeah, and her dog got hit too," added Jimmy

Baxter. "Only Cocoa's not at a dog hospital. He got runned over and he died. I'd be real, real sad if Curly died by a car running over him. I'd even cry if that ever happened—and I never cry now that I'm six." Jimmy hung his head dramatically in grief.

One by one, the other children began sniffling and weeping. Amber suspected tears were going to be a major element in her classroom today. The young teacher was a bit surprised that the students already knew about Cocoa's death but assumed they'd probably heard their own parents discussing the tragedy at home or on the telephone.

In an effort to channel the students' sadness into a positive activity, Amber stood and walked to the center of the classroom. "Mrs. Griffin and I thought it would cheer up Mary Noel if you all made her cards and painted pictures that she can look at in the hospital. I was going to have us work on the messages and pictures after lunch, but I think maybe we'd all feel better if we worked on them right after we take attendance and lunch count and recite the Pledge of Allegiance."

"I'm going to paint a picture of Mary Noel holding Cocoa. She loved him so much. I know because I'm her best friend," Janae rallied long enough to remind everyone of her importance in Mary Noel's life.

"So what! Mary Noel and Cocoa are *my* next-door neighbors, not yours," John Paul Oliveira shouted out abruptly. "I saw the ambulance come pick her up. My mommy was crying so much it made me real sad." The boy's face turned bright red with emotion.

"My Grandpa Bob had to ride in the am-blance when he had a heart 'tack," little Denise Nelson piped up. "It was real loud."

"The heart 'tack was loud?" asked Lily Whitman.

"No! The am-blance was loud," replied Denise.

"Well, your Grandpa Bob didn't die like Cocoa, did he?" John Paul snapped in Denise's direction.

"Children, we must remember our manners. Mary Noel wouldn't want you to be bickering about her. She needs to know we care about her and that we're very sorry about what happened to poor little Cocoa."

Twenty-five expressive little faces nodded at their teacher in agreement. After swiftly taking roll and lunch count and reciting the pledge to the American flag with her students, Amber asked, "Shall we get started on our cards and pictures now?" Once again, mildly enthusiastic nods greeted her eyes.

The next hour was solemn and tranquil in the normally bustling classroom. Mrs. Griffin arrived soon and walked silently through the rows of desks in a show of moral support to Miss Kellen and her students. Amber noted that the principal didn't speak or interrupt the concentration of little hands and minds focused on their very important task.

Amber was grateful for her principal's wisdom

and presence during this difficult situation. As the children completed their projects, they set them on the back table to dry. After a stop at the classroom library's shelves, the students returned to their seats, stoically carrying an array of picture books in their arms. Within a few minutes, everyone had completed their project for Mary Noel and had cleared off their desktops.

As Amber was preparing to move on to the class's reading lesson for the day, the beloved silence was abruptly fractured when the usually bashful Edward Unger hesitantly raised his hand.

"Yes, Edward?"

"Teacher, do dogs go to heaven when they die—you know, like people do?"

CHAPTER TWO

*R*emarkably, Miss Kellen and her students moved through their school day without any more tears or outbursts. The children were not as bubbly and enthusiastic as usual, but they focused on their lessons and completed whatever tasks she gave them.

After class was dismissed, Amber sat at her desk reflecting on the day's events as she organized the paintings and letters the students had made for Mary Noel. The children had certainly created colorful, heartfelt treasures for their injured classmate. More than one of the handwritten greetings brought tears to Amber's eyes. Mary Noel's hospital room walls would no longer be drab and dull.

The young teacher smiled as she slid the important papers into her large denim teacher's tote bag for delivery at the hospital on her way home from school that afternoon. Her parents had presented the monogrammed tote bag to Amber upon her graduation from her masters of education program the previous June. It had a bright red, one-room schoolhouse appliquéd on the front pocket. There was even a real brass bell in the bell tower! The other side of the bag was adorned with a satin-stitched monogram of Amber's initials, ABK. Her middle name, Beatrice, was her parents' tribute to her mother's great aunt who had originally introduced Amber's parents at a church social nearly thirty years ago.

Amber's second stop would be the grocery store. Her cupboards and refrigerator were nearly bare again she thought ruefully. Amber knew she somehow needed to summon up some motivation to create tasty, nutritious meals for herself. While she had enjoyed cooking and baking since she was a teenager, Amber found cooking for one to be so uninspiring. Perhaps if she had someone else to cook for she'd feel more motivated.

Jotting down a few items for a shopping list, Amber slipped into the sleeves of her charcoal gray wool coat and tied her hand-knit, cranberry-hued scarf around her neck. Slipping on the matching hand-knit gloves, Amber hesitated as she visually checked to see that everything was prepared for tomorrow's lessons. Satisfied that all was in order, she grabbed her purse, lunch bag, and the tote bag hosting the greeting cards and paintings for Mary Noel.

As she rushed out to her car, Amber contemplated what she would say to Mary Noel's worried, highly-stressed parents. She had discovered long ago that she dealt much better with difficult situations if she had a firm plan of action. Bowing her head as she sat in the driver's seat of her car, Amber uttered a brief prayer on the Simmons's behalf.

❄ ❄ ❄

When Amber arrived at the hospital, she stopped at the visitor's desk to request Mary Noel's room number. Once she received directions from the teen volunteer, Amber rushed to find the elevator that would take her up to the second floor of the modernized hospital. Uncomfortable in elevators, Amber held her breath as the doors closed and the compartment rose to the second floor. When the bell chimed her arrival at floor two, she waited impatiently for the doors to part so she could exit swiftly and continue on her errand.

Unfortunately, a tall, broad-shouldered man blocked her path as he stood directly in front of the elevator's doors in the hospital hallway. Since the man's back was facing toward the elevator's opening, she figured he wasn't even aware of her presence. Her discomfort grew rapidly when she realized she couldn't exit the windowless compartment. Even when the doors were fully opened, the man didn't budge from his stance. His shoulders and back appeared to be a huge knot of tension. She heard him speaking to someone in dramatic tones. Since she didn't see anyone else nearby, Amber surmised he was talking into a cell phone.

"Excuse me," she said urgently, purposefully trying to sound polite.

There was no response or reaction from the distracted man. Frustrated, she spoke adamantly, this time in a raised voice, "Excuse me, sir!"

This time the man turned around just in time to see the doors of the elevators slide shut. Amber, who had been standing on the threshold of the elevator planning her escape, felt her denim tote bag pull away from her body. She watched as the sliding doors trapped the bag within their firm clutch.

She heard something clatter to the floor. Next, she heard the clicking sound of several buttons on the elevator's operating panel being pushed in rapid succession. The elevator shuddered with a jerk. Fortunately, she'd wisely stayed out of harm's way by stepping back and leaning against the far wall of the elevator. Slowly, the elevator's doors parted once again, and the man stepped through the threshold to greet Amber sheepishly.

"I'm very sorry, miss." He handed her the wrinkled

tote bag with its crumpled contents. "I didn't realize the elevator had arrived. And, uh, well, there's absolutely no excuse for my lack of manners. Are you hurt?" The man's voice and eyes expressed genuine concern.

Amber stood in the elevator gaping at the apologetic man. From the expression he wore and his heartfelt apology, it appeared that he *was* truly sorry about his part in the elevator incident. Realizing she was staring, she said, "No harm done." She smiled to assure him that she harbored no bad feelings toward him. It had always been a priority to Amber to be sure no ill will lingered between her and the people with whom she came into contact within her daily activities.

"I'd feel really bad if you were hurt due to my thoughtlessness."

"No, I'm fine. I think my tote bag took the brunt of the damage." Amber grinned mischievously as she held up the creased bag for inspection. Oily black stains appeared on either side of the bag, lasting proof that the doors had captured her bag.

The chiming of the elevator bell signaled that someone had requested the elevator on a different floor, so the two quickly exited the elevator compartment and stood looking at each other in the stark hallway. Amber was certain she looked anything but attractive with the glaring, institutional-style lighting shining in her eyes. *And exactly why are you worried about how you look right now, Amber?*

"I'm glad you're okay. I don't know what I was thinking—I guess that's the problem. I wasn't thinking. Let's start over. Hi, I'm Paul Watkins." He offered his right hand to Amber hesitantly and seemed relieved when she took it gently with her own gloved hand.

"My name's Amber Kellen." Each held the other's gaze for several moments before a small boy broke between them.

"Hey, mister, is this your phone?" The boy held up the well-used flip phone in question.

"It's mine."

"I saw you drop it when I was waiting for my mom and dad outside my brother's room."

"Thanks a lot, buddy. I don't know what I would have done if you hadn't rescued my phone and me." The boy beamed up at Paul in importance. "Is your brother sick?"

"Yeah, he has ammonia. 'Cept Dr. Adler said Jack's getting better, so he might get to come back home tomorrow."

"Well, pneumonia is serious business. I'm glad Jack's feeling better, but he'll probably need to rest a lot once he gets home. What's your name?"

"I'm Jason. I'm eight and Jack's six. I try hard to take care of him 'cuz he's littler than me, but I don't know how he got ammonia. My dad said it's a really big, bad germ."

"I'll bet you're a great big brother to little Jack.

Hey, I'd like to meet your parents and tell them about your good deed, Jason."

"I'll go get my dad right now!" The boy ran off down the hall before Paul could stop him.

Turning toward Amber, Paul said, "Looks like I've got a new friend. Well, two new friends if I can count you, Amber." When he smiled, she could tell his affection for the boy came naturally.

"Sure. Count me in, Paul. I'd say you really hit it off with Jason too. I'd better be moving along. I have a young friend to visit before visitors' hours end for the evening. It was nice meeting you."

"You're Mary Noel's teacher, aren't you?"

"Yes."

"Tim and Barbara told me how much Mary Noel likes being in your class. I recognize you from church. Believe me, meeting you was the highlight of my day." The two shook hands again briefly and turned their separate ways.

"Thanks. I enjoyed meeting you too."

"Amber," Paul called softly in the empty hallway, "I hope we have a chance to see each other again soon."

The harried teacher turned to face Paul and responded, "I'd like that." His attentive gaze and sincere smile caused Amber to flush with a rush of surprise and a bit of excitement.

❄ ❄ ❄

To his relief, he had finally met Miss Kellen, first-grade teacher extraordinaire. Barbara and Tim had talked at length about Mary Noel's teacher with great admiration since school began. Paul's well-protected psyche quivered in delight from his own brief contact with the amazing Miss Kellen. "She's lovely inside and out. Spending time with her would definitely be worth pursuing."

"Excuse me, mister. My dad says he'll be out to see you in a minute." Paul looked down to discover young Jason staring quizzically up into his face. "What does purr-sue-ing mean? Is it like when a cat purrs?"

Paul chuckled at the boy's definition, which was not far off the mark in this case. "Not exactly, Jason. It's nothing you need to worry about at your age," he grinned down at the youngster fondly.

"Okay, but does lovely mean the same thing as pretty? 'Cuz I don't usually like girls, but I think that lady was *real* pretty."

"Yes, she is," Paul said as his eyes lingered on the door of Mary Noel's room. "She's very pretty."

Just then, a short, athletically built man approached and offered his hand. "I'm Jason's dad, Ralph Webster. Nice to meet you."

"Paul Watkins. It's a pleasure, Ralph. Your son here saved me a lot of time and trouble by returning my cell phone to me. I just wanted to thank you both very much and see if there was anything I could do to repay your kindness."

A broad grin broke out on Ralph's face as he shook his head. "No need for you to repay us. We're just glad Jason took the opportunity to put the Golden Rule into practice." Ralph smiled down affectionately at his son as he drew the boy close. "We teach our boys to help others whenever possible, and I'm really proud Jason could do something meaningful for another person today. Good work, son." He leaned down to ruffle Jason's hair.

"Thanks, Dad."

"I understand your other son is recovering from 'ammonia.'"

Ralph laughed at the use of his older son's vocabulary and said, "He should be able to go home tomorrow, thank goodness. It was touch and go for a while, but the doctors here are just awesome."

"Well, I hope Jack continues to mend and regains his strength soon. It was nice meeting you both. Good luck."

The men shook hands again and Jason waved good-bye as Paul quickly made his way down the hall to Mary Noel's doorway. He could hear Amber's delightful voice talking to Barbara and Tim inside the room. She was asking about Mary Noel's condition and quietly expressed her dismay at the girl's emotional state.

❄ ❄ ❄

"My heart broke into a million pieces when Mrs. Griffin told me the news of the accident this morning before school. I've been so worried all day. Mary Noel's classmates were notably upset too. Especially your little neighbor, John Paul Oliveira. I guess he saw the whole thing."

"It was a shock for the whole neighborhood. We've lived in Apple Blossom since before Mary Noel was born. It was devastating to the man who hit our little girl and her Cocoa." Barbara walked into her husband's warm embrace as she began to weep in earnest.

"Barb, why don't we wait outside and let Miss Kellen have some time with Mary Noel? Maybe hearing her teacher's voice will help her to feel better inside. You know how much our little girl loves her teacher," Mr. Simmons spoke gently to his wife.

"That's a good idea. Miss Kellen, we'll be right outside the door if you need anything."

"I'm sure Mary Noel and I will be just fine." Amber's attempt to be reassuring sounded woefully deficient even to her own ears.

❄ ❄ ❄

Hesitantly, the patient's parents left the room quietly, leaving the new teacher alone with one of her favorite students. Mary Noel's eyes remained tightly closed as if she were trying to shut out all light and color. Amber realized with a jolt that the little girl was likely trying to protect herself from any more hurt.

Amber slowly approached the bed and gently held Mary Noel's small, pale hand in hers. The teacher began speaking softly in soothing tones telling her young student about the day at school. She held up each and every picture in front of Mary Noel's eyes, but unfortunately she garnered no noticeable reaction from the patient.

As Amber read each card aloud, she thought she noticed a faint glimmer of recognition in Mary Noel's facial expression when she read Janae's card. The two girls had been best friends since preschool, and this card was filled with the kind of love and affection communicated only between close friends.

After she had finished reading the cards, Amber began posting the paintings and cards on the walls surrounding Mary Noel's bed. As she taped the papers to the wall, she sang some of the children's favorite songs in an effort to reach out to the injured girl. "You are my sunshine, my only sunshine. You make me happy when skies are gray." On and on Amber sang without any visible response from the patient.

When the tote bag was emptied, Amber once again approached the bedside and held Mary Noel's hand in hers. "Dear Lord, please be with our good friend, Mary Noel, as she heals from her accident. Bless her with good health and peace of mind as her injuries mend. Thank you for your blessings in our lives. Amen."

Gathering her purse and coat, Amber said good-bye and exited the room. She felt awful inside when the girl's parents looked at her with hope and anticipation. "Did she say anything to you or open her eyes?" the girl's father asked apprehensively.

Amber shook her head sadly and told them that she had read the cards and prayed for their daughter. "I hung the pictures on the wall as you asked. The children really did an outstanding job on their cards and paintings. I hope you like them."

"We appreciate everything you've done. Especially your coming here after a long day in the classroom," the young mother offered.

"You're welcome. Please call me if you need anything or if you just want to talk. I'll stop by again tomorrow afternoon on my way home."

"Will you tell your students we said 'thank you' for all of their pretty pictures and cards?" Barbara asked.

"They'll be glad to hear from you." Amber smiled and turned toward the elevator.

❄ ❄ ❄

Paul noticed that the light seemed to have been extinguished in Amber Kellen's eyes as she stepped out of Mary Noel's room and back into the hallway. Worry furrowed the young woman's forehead as she walked away from Tim and Barbara. He would give anything to wipe away the sadness shadowing Amber's eyes, but he'd only just met the woman. Maybe she'd appreciate knowing that he was here to offer support and encouragement to the young girl and her parents.

"Hello again, Miss Kellen."

"Please call me Amber. You make me feel like I'm on playground duty when you call me by my teacher name."

"Sure. How are the Simmonses doing in your opinion?"

Shaking her head sadly Amber spoke quietly, "I haven't known them very long since school began only a few months ago. They both seem really stressed."

"I agree."

"Mary Noel is a special girl, and, to be honest, this tragedy has hit me hard. I had to try to focus on smiling today in front of my students when all I wanted to do was cry."

"I understand. I work for Tim as a journeyman carpenter in his historic renovation business. They've been so good to me over the past several years that I just had to come see what I could do to help out today."

"I'm sure your presence has been a great comfort to the whole family."

"I don't know about that, but it was the least I could do for them."

"I didn't have the heart to ask Mr. or Mrs. Simmons, but has there been any change in Mary Noel's condition since this morning?"

"None that I know of. She either stares off into space or closes her eyes up tight. She's emotionally withdrawn from all communication with anyone. It's tearing Barbara and Tim apart that their daughter won't let them comfort and nurture her."

"I wonder how long this'll go on."

"Tim told me the doctors won't even hazard a guess on how long it will take for Mary Noel to break out of her lethargy."

For the first time that day, Amber allowed her emotions to show through. She soon felt hot tears begin to stream down her face. In an instant, Paul gently pressed a fresh, white cotton handkerchief into her hand.

"Here, use this. Maybe you'll feel better if you let it out. It must have been difficult to play the 'in-control teacher' all day in front of your class."

Amber gazed up at Paul's sienna brown eyes and found kindness and understanding shining through. "Thank you, Paul." She managed to croak out before fresh tears stained her overly warm cheeks. "I didn't realize how hard this had hit me until I was in the room alone with a totally unresponsive Mary Noel. She's usually just so vivacious and talkative, you know?"

"Yes, I do know. Tim often brings her along to the job sites. That girl is a joy to be around, that's for sure." Silence hovered between the two for a few moments before Paul said, "Hey, are you in a hurry or do you have time for a cup of coffee or tea down in the cafeteria?"

Amber's initial reaction was to accept and enjoy Paul's company for a few more minutes. Her logical side told her she had lots to do and that she'd better get going. Her quandary vanished when Paul Watkins gave her a golden smile, appealing to her most vulnerable side. "I'd love a cup of herbal tea. Thanks for suggesting it."

❄ ❄ ❄

An hour and a half later, the two were still talking. Initially, they discussed Mary Noel's condition and their concern for the Simmons family. The conversation transitioned to more personal subjects such as jobs, families, friends, and hobbies. It was a fluid and comfortable conversation. Amber realized with a start that she had never felt so at ease so quickly with any other new acquaintance. Paul was intelligent, witty, and attractive.

His thick, caramel-brown hair would be considered longish by professional standards, but it suited his personality and job as a carpenter. He had a full beard sprinkled with auburn, medium-brown, and a slight touch of gray. She found his deep-set eyes to be exquisitely expressive. When Paul looked at her during their conversation, Amber felt immediately drawn into his circle of warmth and kindness. He was unique when compared with the other men she had dated throughout her college years. Paul seemed transparent in his words and deeds. His sincerity and candor were genuinely refreshing.

Her new acquaintance stood abruptly and pushed his chair under the cafeteria table. "Well, I've kept you away from your list of things to do long enough. Let me walk you out to your car. It's well past dusk now and a parking lot is no place for a lady to be journeying alone after dark."

"Thanks," Amber said as she gathered her things and slid her chair under the table. "I'm not used to having a gentleman around to escort me to my car."

Paul smiled briefly, cupped her elbow in his hand, and guided her through the wide sliding doors of the hospital's main entrance. His presence evoked a sense of security and contentment in Amber that she'd not felt before. *Are you sanctioning this friendship with Paul, Lord? If so, please send me a sign.*

As the two reached her car, Paul stepped closer to Amber and said, "I have a confession to make, Miss Kellen."

Amber froze, half expecting Paul to admit to some major sin he'd committed. Was he an embezzler? Habitual gambler? Tax evader? Or something even worse? Her breath stilled as she awaited his pronouncement. Trying to remain calm inside she tilted her head to one side in question and muttered, "Yes?"

"I've wanted to talk to you since I first saw you. Now that I have—talked to you, that is—I haven't been disappointed. You're even more lovely and delightful than I ever anticipated." He leaned over to gently kiss Amber's cheek before returning to the hospital.

❀ ❀ ❀

Amber touched her cheek where Paul's feather-light kiss had landed. "Was that the sign I had requested earlier?" she whispered aloud as she unlocked her car door. "I hope it was; because, well . . . frankly, I really, truly like this man." She continued speaking aloud as she slid into the stillness of her car's interior. She quickly locked the door and buckled her seat belt before starting her ignition and checking her mirrors.

As she put the car into reverse and slowly began backing up, Amber's heart leapt in her chest when she spied Paul standing in the one empty lane not far from where her car had just been parked. He hadn't walked back to the hospital after all. *Please tell me that Paul didn't just hear me talking about him to myself!* As she passed Paul on her way out to the street he lifted his arm in a friendly wave and smiled knowingly at her. When she glanced back at him in the rearview mirror, Amber was certain she saw him wink at her. *Oh, man, he did hear me!*

CHAPTER THREE

The rest of the week continued in much the same manner. Amber dragged her students through each day's reading, math, spelling, and social studies lessons. Motivating the youngsters to remain on task was a monumental challenge. What alarmed her most was how subdued her students were while playing outside at recess. Mary Noel had been a leader on the playground, and she was sorely missed by her classmates. Nearly every day the class requested time to make cards and letters for Mary Noel. The simple act of expressing their feelings on paper seemed therapeutic for them.

Amber continued to stop by the hospital each afternoon on her way home. Happily, she met up with Paul Watkins in the hallway most days. To her growing dismay, the pair didn't have much of a chance to talk as Paul was somehow managing to do his job as well as Tim's in an effort to keep the company's contracted work on schedule. Amber truly enjoyed Paul's company, and their conversations were comfortable and easy-going. The difference in the rapport between she and Paul was palatable from any she'd previously experienced with a man. "I really like him," she declared aloud as she drove to the hospital one afternoon.

Amber's major concern was that Mary Noel's emotional condition remained unchanged. The girl's bruises, cuts, and scratches were visibly healing. Her broken limbs were mending. The medical staff was worried because Mary Noel still hadn't made any attempt to communicate with anyone, including her parents. The Simmonses were close to inconsolable after several days of their daughter's silence. Amber's heart ached for Barbara and Tim as she read the growing worry and sorrow in their weary eyes each time she saw them. She didn't know what else to do to help the young family except to remember them in prayer and to talk quietly to Mary Noel about the happenings at school.

On one particularly tense afternoon, Amber suggested that they go outside for a walk while she sat with Mary Noel. Tim encouraged his wife to join him outside for a brief respite, and the two left hand in hand. As she bowed her head in prayer and reflection, Amber immediately sensed Paul's presence when he entered the bleak hospital room. As she raised her head, she felt his strong hand squeeze her shoulder reassuringly.

"Any improvement in our little angel?" he asked warily.

"None that I can see," Amber answered sadly. "I sent Barb and Tim out for a walk. They needed a break, and I thought some fresh air and quiet time together would do them some good." Paul squeezed her shoulder again in agreement.

"Amber, I need to talk to you about something sensitive and confidential. I was wondering if we could get together after church on Sunday for a bit. Maybe we can meet at the Country Coffee Café downtown for a light lunch. I'd rather not talk about this at the church."

Her level of curiosity threatened to get the better of her, but she answered calmly. "I don't have any plans after church this week. Should we meet at the café around noon?"

"Sounds good to me. Another thing . . . I'd like." Paul stopped speaking abruptly.

"Yes?" Amber turned toward Paul and their eyes met.

Crimson stained Paul's neckline as he obviously struggled with his own emotions. "Never mind; it wasn't important. I'll see you Sunday at noon if not before. Take care."

❄ ❄ ❄

Amber missed Paul's strength and optimism the moment he exited the room. *I wonder what he wanted to tell me before he stopped talking.* She removed a well-worn copy of the traditional folk tale, "The Gingerbread Man," from her tote bag and began reading it aloud to Mary Noel. All of her first graders were big fans of the naughty little gingerbread man, and she hoped that the story might tug open the oppressive curtain Mary Noel had drawn tightly around herself.

As she read each page, Amber held up the illustrations in front of Mary Noel's shuttered eyes. At the end of the story, the teacher noticed that the girl's eyelids blinked open and then shut again. Was the girl attempting to see the illustrator's renderings, or was it simply an involuntary reaction? Amber decided the girl's reaction was worth mentioning to the Simmonses. They could decide whether to ask the doctor about it.

It was possible that the six-year-old was growing tired of the isolation from her parents and the other caring individuals who visited her room regularly. Amber figured that, by this time, the girl was bored out of her mind. No playing, no drawing, no exercising, no talking. Life must be growing increasingly dull in the world of Mary Noel's self-imposed exile.

❄ ❄ ❄

Amber dressed carefully for church on Sunday morning. The Apple Blossom community was traditional in its dress code for worship and other church functions. It was cold and damp this particular morning, and Amber selected a simple, midnight blue cashmere dress with matching leather belt given to her by her mother a few years earlier. She wore thick, navy blue leggings with her ankle-high, low-heeled black boots. Her long light-brown hair was curled into a feminine style and adorned on the side with a brass hair clip festooned with faux pearls.

As she gathered her bible, purse, and waterproof wraps, Amber's mind once again wandered to Paul and the purpose of their luncheon meeting. *No need to be nervous. It's probably not anything about me. Remember what Mom used to say? "Not everything in the world is about you, Amber."*

The roads were slick with rain, and Amber was grateful that she had allowed extra time to drive to the little country church. The parking lot was nearly full by the time she arrived ten minutes before the service was scheduled to begin. She pulled her raincoat's hood snug over her head and cautiously picked her way over to the church's entrance. She was greeted warmly by the associate pastor, his wife, and their three smiling children. The children attended the school where Amber taught, and, much to the trio's delight, Miss Kellen greeted each youngster by name.

"Miss Kellen, look! I lost a tooth!" exclaimed five-year-old Kimberly.

"Wow, that's quite an accomplishment, Kimberly," the teacher replied warmly.

"I got new shoes," shared seven-year-old Kenny.

"I get to read a bible verse in church this morning," nine-year-old Karen announced proudly.

"Sounds as if the Jones family is having a fantastic morning," Amber said as she shook hands with the pastor and his wife, Beth.

"Yes, they're really feeling their Cheerios this morning. Nice to see you again, Amber," Pastor Jones offered before Amber moved into the sanctuary for worship.

Much to her surprise, Paul was standing beside the archway of the sanctuary. "Good morning. Okay if we sit together this morning? I mean, that is, if you don't object to being seen with me." Paul was fidgeting nervously as he gazed intently into Amber's hazel eyes.

"I'd love to sit with you." She smiled up into his strained face. She was rewarded with a dazzling smile.

"Great. You choose the pew." He gestured for Amber to walk ahead of him.

It felt so peculiar to be escorted down the aisle of the small church by a man. Amber was in the habit of sitting by herself, but she found herself energized by the thought of sharing the worship service with Paul.

The minister's sermon was titled "God First;

Others Second." The themes of the message were kindness and compassion. Amber was inspired by the church leader's poignant words. After Pastor Harris's lesson and a lovely singing duet were completed, Paul leaned over and whispered, "That sermon was just what I needed to hear this morning."

Amber nodded subtly in agreement as the congregation stood to sing the final hymn. After the benediction, she led the way out of the pew and headed to the church's doorway to greet the pastor.

"Good morning, Amber. It's great to see you at our little church again," Pastor Harris smiled wisely as he shook her hand. "We'd love to have you as a member of our congregation."

"Thank you for the invitation, Pastor Harris. I'll probably take you up on your offer." She smiled and moved on to greet Mrs. Harris.

❄ ❄ ❄

Paul shook Pastor Harris's hand and lowered his voice. "How's it going, Paul? You look like the cat that ate the canary. Any reason for that big smile other than the fact that you're in the presence of a lovely young woman this morning?" The pastor's face wrinkled in good humor.

"I was inspired by your message, Pastor. God's goodness is becoming easier for me to spot in my own life."

"Yes, and the Lord knows what each of His children needs," the pastor said firmly. A look of understanding passed silently between the two men.

Lowering his voice, the pastor said loud enough for only Paul's ears, "You'll be in my prayers, son."

"I'd appreciate that, Pastor. Thank you."

The rainstorm had passed through, and the morning was filled with a fresh, cool breeze and brilliant skies. As the congregants milled around outside on the church's courtyard, Amber broke away to speak with some other families that she knew. Paul chatted with a couple of the guys who also worked for Simmons Construction about an upcoming project.

As he scanned the crowd, Paul spotted a tall man swiftly maneuvering his way over to Amber. "Todd Crocker," Paul said aloud with a scowl. He should have known he wasn't the only man interested in Amber Kellen.

"What was that, Paul?" one of his coworkers asked.

"Nothing. I'll see you guys tomorrow. Enjoy your Sunday afternoon with your families." Paul strode determinably over to where Amber was engaged in conversation with Todd.

"No, I'm sorry. I have other plans for lunch today. I appreciate the invitation, though," she said patiently.

"How about next weekend? I'm free Friday night, Saturday night, or Sunday afternoon—your choice. I'd really like to take you out so we can get to know each other. You're lucky because I've had my eye on you ever since you moved to Apple Blossom," Todd said.

Before she had a chance to respond to Todd, Paul stepped up to the group and stood next to Amber. Relief washed across her feminine features as she glanced over at him. He guessed that she was firmly entrenched in the awkward position of not knowing how to kindly, but effectively, brush off Todd's unwanted attention. He saw a wobbly smile cross her mouth as she searched for the right words.

Acknowledging Todd with a nod of his head, Paul glanced at Amber and said, "Ready to head for the restaurant?"

"Yes, I'm ready. Thank you."

"Oh, so that's how it is, huh?" Todd ground out the words bitterly. "You two together as a couple? Well, you'll come crawling back to me once you get to know him. He's not half the man I am. You just wait and see." Todd turned on his heels and trotted off toward the parking lot.

"That did *so* not go well." The falter in Amber's voice alerted Paul that she had been shaken by Todd's words and brusque manner.

"It's not about you. That's just how Todd is and always has been. I went through junior high and high school with him. This is how he always handles rejection. You should have seen how he reacted when he didn't make the high school's baseball team. Nothing you could have said or done would have changed his reaction. Trust me." Paul gently squeezed her elbow in support.

His touch warmed Amber's soul. "I just feel so awful; I hate hurting people's feelings."

"There's nothing that says you have to accept every date that's offered to you. You were polite when you turned him down."

"I know, but he walked away mad, and that really bothers me."

"Try not to let Todd's words ruin your day."

"I won't. I've been looking forward all week to spending time with you today."

"Really? Thanks. Are you ready to go now? You can follow me if you want." Paul smiled down at Amber and felt fortunate he was the man she was sharing lunch with today.

"Let me say good-bye to my friend, Joanne. Then we can go." Amber walked over to a professionally dressed, middle-aged woman who was speaking with another couple.

Paul saw the two women embrace warmly, and he felt a pang of longing to be the one on the receiving end of Amber's attention. *Get your mind back on track, Watkins. This lunch is not a date. You're meeting with Amber solely for business purposes. And if you believe that, I have some swampland up at the North Pole that I'd be glad to sell you really cheap.* Paul heard himself chuckle at his own conscience's recrimination of his motives for inviting Amber to lunch.

❄ ❄ ❄

The Country Coffee Café was a quaint, old-fashioned diner decorated in mid-century memorabilia with soft music of the fifties and sixties piping through the speakers above the red and black vinyl booths. Paul had been enjoying the delicious home-cooked fare since he was a small boy. His luncheon favorite was the chicken fried steak with mashed potatoes and gravy, and corn on the cob or fresh baked green bean casserole. Sometimes when he was really hungry, he ordered both of the vegetable dishes. The diner's homemade buttermilk biscuits drowning in real butter were an added attraction in his mind. Yes, this meal was a real artery-clogger, according to the latest health news reports.

Amber arrived a few minutes after Paul and parked her small hybrid car next to his truck at the front of the lot. As he helped her debark her car, he was once again struck by this woman's subtle inner and outer beauty. How any man could not notice Amber's natural radiance was beyond him. He was thrilled to be spending this time with her, even though the subject matter of their discussion was not appealing.

Once they were seated, Paul introduced Amber to his favorite waitress. Hazel had watched him grow up over the years and had never failed to make him feel like the most special boy, now man, in the entire diner. Hazel's warmth reached out to Amber, and soon the two were chatting like old friends. It seemed as if Amber just had that kind of positive effect on people. Paul realized with a start that he included himself in that particular observation.

"Give us a few minutes, will you please, Hazel?" Paul asked.

Hazel giggled. "As if you'll ever choose anything but the chicken fried steak with mashed potatoes and gravy, both veggie sides, and a chocolate brownie sundae for dessert, Paul Sampson Watkins." The echo of Hazel's giggles could be heard as she wandered over to another table.

"Sampson?" Amber's eyebrows were raised in question, and a mischievous grin lurked behind her relaxed facial features.

"Uh, Sampson was my mother's maiden name."

"Oh, I thought maybe you were named after Sampson of biblical fame."

"Definitely not," Paul could feel himself blushing at his neckline. "Can we kindly change the subject, please?"

"Certainly. What do you want to talk about?"

"That was a great sermon this morning, wasn't it?"

Amber nodded in agreement. "Pastor Harris is good at reminding us how our words and deeds affect the world around us. His lessons are practical too. I always feel uplifted at that church."

"I feel the same way. He always talks about something *I* need to hear."

Hazel approached the table with her pad and pencil and waited patiently while Amber placed her order for a ham and cheese omelet, warm blueberry muffin, and pot of herbal tea.

"What'll it be, young man? Come on. Surprise me," Hazel chided with a bright smile.

"Give me the usual, Hazel," Paul replied, snapping his plastic menu closed with exaggerated flourish before flashing a dramatic wink in Hazel's direction.

Paul heard the delightful tinkling sound of Amber's laughter before he got caught up in her animated smile—a sound and sight he could gladly live with for many, many years to come.

After Hazel's audible sigh and dramatic departure from the table, Amber said, "Hazel's got your number for sure."

"Yes, she does. She and my mother actually grew up together here in Apple Blossom. They were best friends in high school and kept in contact through the years. Hazel's been a big encouragement to me since my mother passed away almost five years ago. All kidding aside, Hazel is someone I can count on to be there for me if I need her assistance and guidance."

"How wonderful it must be to have someone like Hazel in your life."

Paul nodded, and then became quiet and serious. "Do you mind if I change the subject?"

Amber tilted her head to one side to signal her acquiescence to his request.

"The reason I wanted to meet with you privately is to talk about the Simmonses." Paul paused briefly, as if gathering his thoughts. "Tim mentioned recently how fast their hospital bills are adding up. I couldn't believe how hefty the basic daily costs were when he told me. Every little item adds up super fast. It's mind-blowing actually."

"Do they have any medical insurance?"

"Yes, they have a modest policy through Tim's company. The problem is that the co-payments and deductibles are really high. Tim and Barbara have no idea how they'll pay the bills. Since Mary Noel's mental condition is not improving at all, the doctors don't even know when she'll be able to go home. In the meantime, the costs that they're responsible for are adding up quickly."

"I've heard of situations like this. Is there anything I can do to help out? I mean, I have my own student loans to pay off, but I may be able to contribute one hundred dollars each month."

Wanting to connect with this kind woman, Paul reached across the table to cradle Amber's small hands in his larger, calloused hands. Leveling his gaze at her, Paul said, "That's generous of you. When I said 'hefty' for the hospital bills, I guess what I really meant was 'astronomical.' Every bandage, every injection, every night's stay, every dose of medicine, every sponge bath, every doctor's visit is charged at an ultra-high rate. I don't know what the exact number is, but this could ruin Barb and Tim for years to come." He shook his head in despair.

"I'll do whatever I can to help the Simmonses. Let's brainstorm some ideas and find a way we can make a positive contribution to this cause." She squeezed his hands reassuringly. Their eyes met, and Amber smiled empathetically.

"Good idea. I feel better just knowing you'll help me out with this. I really feel badly for Mary Noel. I don't know how I'd handle it if I witnessed Dallas's death."

"Dallas?" Amber asked quietly.

"My golden retriever. We've been buddies for over six years now. He's the best dog ever."

At that moment, Hazel bustled over to the table with a pot of tea and a large glass of iced tea. "The rest of your order'll be comin' up in a few!" Hazel called out to them over her shoulder as she hurried down the aisle to greet some more diners.

Reluctantly, Paul released Amber's hands and immediately missed the warmth he'd enjoyed from this simple connection. When his gaze once again met Amber's, she had a new expression on her face he'd not seen from her before.

"What is it?" he asked hesitantly.

"You're amazing, Paul. Tim and Barbara have a problem, and even though you're running his company and working hard at your own job, you're taking the initiative to help them out. I admire you for your compassion and your can-do attitude. They say the world is divided into two groups. Doers and thinkers. I've always been a 'doer.' Seems as if you might be a 'doer' too."

❄ ❄ ❄

Amber sensed Hazel's positive energy before she saw the waitress swiftly coming near with a loaded tray. "Here we are, you two. Amber, your omelet and muffin. Please let me know if everything is cooked to your liking." Hazel turned and smiled lovingly at Paul. "Your usual, Mr. Watkins. Enjoy your lunch."

The pair said, "Thank you, Hazel," in unison as the waitress sped off to accomplish her next task.

"Let's say a blessing before we eat," Paul suggested.

Amber nodded in agreement, and he began speaking softly. For the next little while, the two ate in comfortable silence. After they both had cleared their plates, Amber brought out a small writing pad and pen from her purse.

"I'll jot down some ideas while we talk."

"Good idea."

"I think that, considering the amount of money needed to cover the hospital bills, it's safe to say we are going to need to get a lot of people involved in this, right?"

Paul nodded enthusiastically. "The more people who get involved, the faster we can solve this problem."

"How about if we have a community fund-raiser? A fun activity or event for families to attend together so everyone would really get behind the idea of donating their hard-earned dollars to help out the Simmons family?"

"I like the idea of a family event. We already have a lot of fund-raisers in town where various organizations are selling items like cookies, calendars, wreaths, and garlands . . . that sort of thing. People in this community support things as much as they can."

"Good to know. I think a family festival would be successful, but we need a 'catchy' theme. I've heard the town already has a carnival in the spring and a county fair in the summer." Amber looked at Paul for confirmation.

"Yes, and then there's the Founder's Day Celebration in the early autumn. It's a kind of harvest festival with scarecrows and agricultural displays."

Tapping the pen rhythmically on her hand, Amber broke the silence, "When does it begin snowing around here?"

"Usually we have a few inches right around Thanksgiving, but that obviously didn't happen this year. We usually get two or three feet by mid-December. Though, with global warming, it's hard to tell what might happen this year. The winter before last was the warmest winter on record across the nation."

"I understand all that factual, logical stuff. But steadfast, unwavering faith is what we truly need in this situation. A belief that the details will work out to create an environment for a miracle to blossom."

Both were silent for several minutes. "I can almost see those gears and wheels turning in that imaginative mind of yours. What're you thinking?"

"This idea is still in the sprout stage. I was thinking we could have a snow festival. Sleigh rides, a snowman-building contest, snowball-throwing contests, snowshoe relays, hot food and drink stands, that sort of thing. Families would pay an admission fee to attend and then pay for the extras like the food and beverages and special activities. We can get the vendors to donate a large portion of their receipts to the medical expenses fund, say seventy or seventy-five percent *after* their expenses."

"That's an awesome idea. We could get the local newspaper and radio stations to give us some free advertising. Maybe we could draw in families from the surrounding counties too. People are always searching for something fun to do in the cold weather. I think if we're lucky we could collect a couple of thousand dollars to help out the Simmonses. Let's do it!"

"I'd like to have the festival right before Christmas Day. Like a community-wide holiday celebration. We could ask Pastor Harris if we can advertise using the church's social media accounts. You know, post an announcement on the church's Facebook page and send out some tweets about the festival details from the church's Twitter account. Then as the date of the festival draws closer, we could amp up the tweets and Facebook postings. I think the church also sends out newsletters to the congregation via email to keep people updated on events."

"I like all of those ideas. Write them down on our list of things to do."

Amber worked silently for a few minutes, putting their thoughts down on paper for future reference. When she was finished writing, she looked up at Paul with a grin. "This might just work."

"I think that we should keep all of this to ourselves for now. We'll share our plans with Tim and Barb when we have all the details worked out. How about we think about this for a couple more days and then get together on Tuesday night for dinner. What do you think? Would you like to go out to dinner with me?"

Paul's puppy-dog eyes looked so hopeful that before Amber had time to conjure up a list of reasons why she should *not* go out to dinner with him, she heard her own voice responding cautiously, "Okay."

"Great! I'll pick you up at six o'clock sharp at your place. Dress casually, but warmly. And bring your notebook." Paul grinned broadly as he pulled a crisp ten-dollar bill out of his wallet and placed it under the ketchup bottle for Hazel's tip. Then he slid out of the diner's booth and helped Amber bundle up in her coat and scarf before gliding over to the cash register to settle their bill.

"Here, let me pay for my—"

"No way, young lady. This is my treat." Paul beamed at her.

In that moment, Amber felt her heart flutter joyfully. *I certainly hope I'm reading these signs correctly . . .*

CHAPTER FOUR

*A*mber and Paul individually continued to visit Mary Noel and her parents in the hospital each day. There was no noticeable improvement in the little girl's mental or emotional condition, but the medical staff assured the Simmonses that their little girl was healing up physically at a very encouraging pace.

"We're so grateful to you, Miss Kellen, for being so devoted to our little girl," Barbara Simmons said tearfully on Monday afternoon.

Amber patted Barbara's trembling hand and smiled warmly. "Your Mary Noel is a special little girl. We all want to see her happy and healthy again as soon as possible. I'd really like you to call me Amber."

"Okay. Feel free to call us Barbara and Tim," she said with a weak smile. "I'm going to be blunt here,

Amber. Tim and I are worried that Mary Noel is still not talking to us. She's been our cute little chatterbox since she started talking at twenty months old. The doctors feel she would be much better off sharing her experiences and pain with us. But how do we get through to her?"

"I believe Mary Noel feels your love and prayers. She just doesn't know how to deal with her grief over losing little Cocoa. We need to remember she's only six years old, and her mind works very differently than an adult's."

"You're right, of course. It's just difficult to remember that each day." The young mother's vacant eyes reflected her fatigue, sadness, and grief.

"I'll visit again tomorrow after school. Is there anything I can bring to you or your family?" Amber reached for Barbara's trembling hand.

"I had a thought last night when I couldn't sleep, and I wanted to share it with you. I wonder if we should have a coloring book and box of crayons on hand in case Mary Noel decides she wants to draw or color. Those were her two favorite activities before . . ."

"What an excellent idea! I'll stop at the drug store and pick up both of those items plus a little pad of drawing paper and a package of stickers. We can put them in a basket on her bed. Maybe by having these things close by, she'll at least be inspired to open her eyes. At best, maybe she'll start using them to express herself."

❄ ❄ ❄

Tuesday afternoon Amber stopped by the hospital for a brief visit. As always, Mary Noel remained unresponsive as Amber read and talked to her. Before leaving, Amber set out a sky-blue basket on the bed alongside Mary Noel. She spoke aloud as she placed the coloring book, drawing pad, and box of crayons in the basket. She slid a package of colorful animal stickers on top.

"I brought along a few things I thought you might like to have while you're in the hospital, Mary Noel. I know how much you like to draw and color, so here's a brand-new coloring book, a crisp drawing pad, and a box of bright crayons with thirty-two of your favorite colors inside. Oh, I almost forgot. Here's a package of cute stickers too. You can draw, color, write, or even just scribble if you want. Take care, little one." She patted the little girl on the hand and turned to leave the room.

As Amber approached the door, she heard a slight rustling behind her and turned around just in time to see Mary Noel leafing through the items in the basket. The youngster wore a timid smile. She slipped out the door without saying anything. Mary Noel would communicate with those around her when she was ready.

"How is she?" Tim asked anxiously as they met in the hallway.

Putting her finger to her lips, Amber motioned for the girl's parents to follow her to the waiting area at the end of the hall.

"I don't want us to get excited about what I just observed, but I thought you should know what your daughter just did."

The couple leaned forward and hung onto every word Amber said before melting into each other's arms. As she walked away from them, she heard Tim murmuring words of comfort and support to his weeping wife. She overheard Barbara say, "Maybe she's turned the corner."

When the doors to the elevator slid closed, Amber closed her eyes and gave a silent prayer of thanksgiving. Then she got out her pad and jotted down a few more ideas about the snow festival. She felt a jolt of excitement when she remembered that tonight was her dinner date with Paul.

❄ ❄ ❄

Amber rushed home to relax for a few minutes before getting ready. She was settling down for a cup of warm herbal tea when her cell phone chimed. Paul's brief text read, "Are we still on for dinner at six?" Amber smiled at his use of full words for his message. Most people nowadays simply typed abbreviations and numerals for their text communications. The rules of "text-speak" went against Amber's orderly teacher's mind.

"I'm looking forward to it. See you in a while."

A minute later her phone chimed again. "Can't wait to see you."

Although she was alone, Amber felt herself blush from her collar bone up to her scalp. This man made her feel sensations she'd never felt before. She remembered Paul had told her to dress casually, but she wanted to look really pretty for her date. Leaving her cup of tea on the kitchen counter, she rushed into her bedroom to search for just the right outfit to wear tonight. It was her first official date with Paul Watkins, and she wanted to pay tribute to its significance by dressing up in something attractive.

Amber finally settled on a pair of black wool slacks, a long-sleeved, dark rose sweater, and a silk neck scarf with swirls of colorful stripes in aqua, violet, and rose. She carefully curled her hair into a pony tail gathered at her neck with a black velvet scrunchie. Half an hour later, Amber added some dangling earrings made of turquoise and set in silver and a sleek cuff bracelet to match. The unique set had been a Christmas gift from her parents last year.

Amber zipped on her low-heeled black boots and laid out a short black wool jacket and black cashmere gloves. Checking her watch, she realized she had just ten minutes to spare until Paul arrived. She sat down to finish her tea and then straightened up her living area and kitchen in case her date wanted a tour of her humble abode.

❄ ❄ ❄

At the stroke of six, Paul arrived carrying a festive wicker basket filled with a pot of brilliant deep purple hothouse violets. A jaunty, bright-yellow florist's bow adorned the basket's handle.

"These are for you, Amber, in honor of our first official date. The start of what I hope will lead to many happy times together." He smiled as he placed the basket in her outstretched hands.

"What a fun surprise! Thank you. I don't know what to say except thank you. Would you like to sit down for a few moments before we leave for dinner? How did you know that violets are my favorite flowers?"

"I cannot tell a lie, ma'am. I had no clue that you liked violets. I really just tried to find a gift that would not pale next to your natural beauty. These flowers reminded me of you—cheerful and lovely."

Amber was speechless. Was Paul serious or was he simply teasing her? One look at his eyes told her he held her in high esteem. "I don't know what to say except thank you so much. Would you like to sit down for a few moments before we leave for dinner?"

He quickly glanced at his watch and said, "We

have a reservation for six thirty, so I think we have a few minutes to talk." He followed her gesture and sat in a dark-blue recliner as Amber sat across from him on a matching sofa. "By the way, did I mention how nice you look this evening?"

Amber lowered her head bashfully and said, "You're spoiling me, but thanks."

"My pleasure. I hope you're hungry. We're going to the Blue Moon Steak House just across the county line in Moose Hill."

"Oh, I've heard wonderful things about that restaurant! I haven't eaten there yet, but some of the teachers at school said it's a really nice place. When you took me out to the Country Coffee Café, it was the first time I'd eaten out since I moved here."

"I guess you're probably busy with your schoolwork in the evenings and on weekends."

"Yes, I do paperwork a lot in the evenings. I spend weekends doing my laundry, housework, and grocery shopping. I haven't been out much, because, truthfully, I don't really have any friends. You're the first person who has reached out to me. I mean, the other teachers and staff at school have been friendly and helpful, but they're all married with children. They don't have time to be carting me around."

"I'm amazed. I thought you'd have had a long line of suitors waiting at the door to take you out." Paul sounded incredulous.

"You're the first man who has asked me out since I moved here. Well, I guess Todd Crocker was the very first, but by then you had already captured my interest." Amber slapped her hand against her mouth, aghast that she had actually spoken her thoughts aloud. "I'm so sorry. You didn't ask for a full confession, and I don't usually speak so frankly."

"My name's Paul, not Frank." He smiled broadly and reached for her hand. "I'm flattered by your words, Amber. Since we're confessing, I'm grateful that you gave me the first chance to date you since you've become an Apple Blossomer."

"Apple Blossomer?"

"That's what the locals here call an accepted newcomer."

"Charmed, I'm sure," she said, batting her eye-lashes coquettishly.

Paul threw his head back and laughed heartily, inciting a fit of giggling from Amber. Once they had collected their composure, the two looked at each other curiously for a few silent moments.

"Would you like the grand tour of my little mansion?"

"Sure."

For the next few minutes, she humorously guided Paul through her two bedroom apartment. There really wasn't much to see, but Amber embellished her tour with as many adjectives and adverbs as she could summon on a moment's notice. Soon her guest checked his watch and signaled that it was time to leave for the restaurant. In his truck, Amber patted her purse and told Paul she'd brought her notebook along so they could discuss all of her finely tuned ideas for Mary Noel's fund-raiser.

❄ ❄ ❄

The couple was greeted by a hostess at the doors of the Blue Moon Steak House. They were soon seated at an elegant table covered in a midnight blue linen tablecloth with a moon and stars pewter candleholder at the center. The glow of the flickering candle created a cozy ambience that Amber appreciated.

"This is really nice," Amber gushed as she gazed at the Vincent Van Gogh reproduction art hanging on the walls. "I've always admired Van Gogh's work."

"I thought you'd like it here. The food's good too." Paul smiled at Amber fondly.

After ordering their meals, the pair exchanged more details about their families and respective upbringings. Paul was an only child while Amber was the eldest of three girls. She was from Southern California, and he was a hometown boy.

"I guess this winter will be a shock to your system with you being a sunny Southern California girl and all," Paul said.

"I think I'll be just fine. I spent more than a few

winter vacations at my grandparents' cabin in Colorado. My dad taught me how to drive in the snow when I was a teenager, and I don't mind a little chill in the air. In fact, I actually prefer cold weather to the dry SoCal heat."

"Let me know if you need anything when the winter weather begins. I know where you can get some excellent snow tires for a good price."

"I may take you up on that."

"Wanna talk about the fund-raiser while we wait to be served?" Paul asked.

Amber immediately opened her purse and presented her notebook and pen for Paul's approval. "I remembered that Mary Noel loves angels. She writes about them, draws them, and talks about them a lot. She really wanted to be an angel in the church's Christmas pageant this year too."

"Doesn't look as if that particular wish will come true this Christmas," Paul said sadly.

"No, it won't. But I got to thinking—why not make the purpose of this festival two-fold?"

"How so?" Paul asked with his eyebrows knit together in puzzlement.

"The main purpose is to raise funds for the medical bills, right?"

"Of course." Paul wasn't entirely certain he knew where this was leading, but he was willing to listen to Amber's thoughts.

"The second purpose can be to raise Mary Noel's spirits and perhaps pull her out of her depression better than any medication or psycho-therapy can do."

"I'm with you. Keep talking."

He could see Amber was excited about sharing her ideas since she leaned forward to continue. "Let's call the festival, 'Angels for Mary Noel.' All the elements of the festival will involve angels as much as possible. For example, we can have a snow angel contest for the kids along with a children's choir singing songs like 'Hark the Herald Angels Sing' and 'Angels We Have Heard on High.' The cookies sold at the food booth could be sugar cookies cut out in the shape of an angel. We can sell warm sweatshirts printed with an angel motif and the slogan, 'Angels for Mary Noel' for people to wear to the festival."

"I'll rustle up some volunteers to build a few large plywood angel cutouts and fill them with white lights and a sign that reads, 'Angels for Mary Noel.' Like you said before, we could have vendors selling hot chocolate, coffee, and tea," Paul said. "People will really go for this type of festival. It's wholesome holiday fun that helps out another local family. Great thinking!"

"Thank you, but we still have loads of work to do to make this become reality. If we're going to hold the festival before Christmas, we only have three weeks to pull everything together. Before we go any further with our plans, I think we should talk with Tim and Barbara to be sure that it's all right with them if we go forward with the fund-raiser. I don't want them to be embarrassed about having other people contribute money to pay their bills."

Paul rubbed his chin, deep in thought. "I agree with you. I'll speak to Tim privately and let him talk it over with Barbara. Let's keep this to ourselves until we get the go ahead from the Simmonses."

"I'll sketch out some more details in case they do agree with our ideas for the fund-raiser."

The waitress arrived with their salads and beverages on a large tray and began setting dishes and glasses on the table. "Steaks'll be done in a few more minutes, folks."

"Thank you." After the waitress walked away, Paul asked, "Shall I say grace?"

"Yes, please."

After Paul's blessing, the pair began eating their salads while chatting quietly about inconsequential things. Amber suddenly said, "Oh, I almost forgot to tell you! While I was looking through some school records, I noticed that Mary Noel's seventh birthday is on Christmas Eve. I thought that might be a great day to hold the festival. It's a Saturday, and we could schedule the activities to be open for a few hours in the afternoon. Then people will still have time to go home to eat dinner and go to their Christmas Eve church services. What do you think?"

"December twenty-fourth sounds fantastic. I'll tell Tim when I talk to him."

The rest of their meal was served, and the two found they never lacked topics of conversation. They covered a lot of subjects during their first official date. When they were ready to leave the restaurant, Paul realized with great regret that he was not ready to say good night to Amber so soon.

"Want to go for a drive?" he suggested. "I can show you some of the outlying scenery surrounding downtown Apple Blossom along with several important sites that are essential for any local school teacher to visit."

Amber chuckled. "I'd like that. I haven't had a tour of my new hometown yet."

"It's cold outside. Would you like me to order a cup of coffee or tea for you to take along in my truck?"

"Herbal tea would be a welcomed treat."

He called over the waitress and ordered two herbal teas to go. The waitress returned shortly with the bill and their take-out order. Paul left a tip for the waitress along with enough money to cover their bill. He helped Amber with her coat and proceeded to hold the restaurant door open as they exited the fine restaurant.

Paul opened the truck door for Amber and waited for her to be seated. "I really enjoyed our dinner. Thank you." She smiled, and Paul instinctively responded by leaning into the truck and kissing her on the cheek.

"You're most welcome, pretty lady," he blurted out confidently.

Amber gently touched her cheek. He closed the passenger door firmly and made his way around the front of the truck to his door. After placing the beverages on the console, Paul settled into his seat.

Amber was holding her palm over the spot on her cheek where he'd kissed. The two gazed at one another and laughed quietly. "This is my most fun first date ever, Paul."

"I'm sure it doesn't have anything to do with me," he teased in an effort to get Amber to laugh again. He really loved her laugh.

"I must admit you have made a *little* bit of a positive impression on me, Mr. Watkins," she said with a soft giggle.

Upon hearing the sincerity and affection in Amber's voice, he sensed that something unique was in store for the two of them. He didn't know how deeply their relationship would develop or how long it would last, but he had the distinct feeling that a strong and positive bond would grow between them.

"Now please understand that touring good old

Apple Blossom is not quite the same as going on a tour of say New York City or Los Angeles. However, we do have several sites not to be missed by the discriminating newcomer. First, we'll drive by the town's original water tower."

"Water tower?" Amber gazed at him with a humorous glint in her eyes.

"Yes, it's the Harry S. Truman Memorial Water Tower. A very important monument to our nation's colorful thirty-second President."

The couple drove back to Apple Blossom while chatting about their favorite books, music groups, and songs. Soon the truck slowed noticeably and Paul pointed out the side window.

"A-a-a-a-and, here we are." Paul pulled to a stop beside a small metal tank sitting directly on the ground next to the local municipal utilities office. The tank was only about four feet high and just about as wide.

"It's so small!" Amber exclaimed.

"Well, that's because this is a replica of the original water tower installed at this site in 1950. It collapsed in a bad snowstorm one winter. This one is only here because they have a plaque mounted on that post right over there. The good citizens of Apple Blossom didn't want to remove the plaque, as they felt it would be disrespectful to Plain Speaking Harry. The new and functional water tower is huge and is about a quarter of a mile that direction."

Amber giggled at Paul's histrionics. "Too bad I don't have my camera with me," she deadpanned.

"I must warn you, this tour only gets more exciting from here on out. Next we'll visit the Franklin Delano Roosevelt covered bridge."

"I didn't know we have a covered bridge here. They're so quaint and nostalgic. I always think of the colonial period when I see a covered bridge."

"Don't get your hopes up now. This one's not your typical covered bridge."

"Oh?"

"There it is just ahead there on your left. Don't blink or you might miss it."

"I don't see it."

"Let me pull closer and shine my headlights on it."

As he maneuvered the truck closer, his headlights shone on a small shed with a glass door and a large picture window to the right. Inside the shed was a table with a light shining on a wooden model of some sort of structure.

"What is it?" Amber sounded puzzled.

"Let's get out and go look."

The couple exited the truck and met in the headlights' beams. Paul grabbed Amber's hand and led her over to the shed. Inside the building was a finely crafted model of an exquisite wooden bridge mounted on a simple wooden stand. She turned her head back toward Paul in bewilderment.

"The government ran out of the money to fund this type of project once World War II began. So all we have left to remind us of the FDR covered bridge is this model built by one of the town's master craftsmen in 1940 when the idea of the bridge was originally proposed."

"It's an amazing model. Look at all that detail."

Paul twirled Amber back around and rushed toward the truck. "Brrrr, it's cold tonight. You may want to sip some tea on the way to the next landmark."

"You mean there are more fabulous sites to see this evening?"

"You betcha. Last, but not least, we'll visit the Dwight D. Eisenhower Memorial Swimming Pool. Better known around here as the 'I Like Ike Swim Hole.'"

Amber sipped her hot tea as Paul took the wheel. It seemed as if they were driving around in circles when all of a sudden Paul pulled up in front of a fenced-off pond with weeds growing around the edges. Flicking on his high beams, he said, "We don't need to get out to admire this monument."

"You said it was a swimming pool, but this just looks like a dirty old mud hole."

Paul laughed heartily before turning toward Amber. "You're learning. Things are not always what they seem here in Apple Blossom. This was a hare-brained idea hatched by a group of local teens back in the early 1960s. As you can see, it wasn't very successful."

"Did people actually swim here?"

"No, no, no. In an effort to save the town some money, the teens volunteered to dig a hole that would eventually become a community swimming pool. Once the boys began digging, they discovered fairly quickly how difficult a job it would be to dig out a full-sized swimming pool. They worked for three full days in the blazing summer sun and only got this far before giving up entirely. Mind you, they used shovels and trowels, not heavy-duty, earth-moving equipment."

"How do you know the history of this site so well?"

"My dad was one of the nutty teens who worked on the project. He went on to become a well-respected, skilled civil engineer. He lives and works in New York City now."

"Is there a community pool for Apple Blossomers to use?"

"Over in the next county there's an Olympic-sized public pool. As they say in Sunday school, 'Thus endeth the lesson for today.'"

"Well, I guess I should thank you for the intriguing tour."

"Yes, you should. Now you're well versed enough in our community's history that you can teach your class all about Apple Blossom of yesteryear. Ready to head home? If you don't mind my saying so, you look really cold."

"I guess we should head back. I sure hate for the evening to end, but I need some rest for school tomorrow."

❄ ❄ ❄

At Amber's front door, Paul drew her close and kissed her on the cheek again. "I really enjoy spending time with you," he whispered into her ear.

"I love being with you too," she responded softly.

"Would you like to go out with me again this Saturday night? We could go back over to Moose Hill to see a movie or go to a coffee house I know where people play live folk and Christian music. We can get a bite to eat first."

"I love music. The coffee house sounds like fun."

Smiling into her hair, Paul said, "I'll pick you up at five o'clock on Saturday. I'm going to talk to Tim tomorrow, so I should have some news about their feelings to share with you that evening."

"Don't forget that if you're too busy to call during the day, you can text me with updates."

"Will do."

Stepping back so that she could look Paul in the eyes, Amber said, "Thank you for everything. This was truly the most fun I've ever had on a date. I'll think of you and our date each time I look at those beautiful violets you gave me."

Paul nodded at her kind words and then said, "I'd better get going. If I don't leave now, I'll keep you out here in the cold talking for another few hours. Good-bye, Amber. Thanks for being my date for the evening. I had a great time too." He kissed her again on the cheek and waited while she stepped inside her apartment.

The two waved silently to each other before Amber closed and locked her front door. As she peeked out her front window, she saw Paul heading back to his truck. He took off as soon as he buckled his seat belt. Amber leaned on the inside of her front door and said, "Awesome."

CHAPTER FIVE

*A*mber's week passed by quickly as she anxiously anticipated seeing Paul again on Saturday night. She was unable to visit Mary Noel on
Wednesday due to a staff meeting, but she stopped by
with new pictures and letters on Thursday and Friday
afternoon. Tim told her that Paul was swamped at
work trying to finish several projects before the bad
weather set in for good. Not seeing Paul for three
days made Saturday afternoon seem off in the dis-
tant future, but she felt if a long-term relationship
was in God's plan for their lives, it would happen in
good time.

Friday afternoon Amber's phone chimed. She
was ecstatic to see a text message from Paul. It read,
"Talked to Tim and Barb. Good news for Angels for

Mary Noel. Counting the minutes until 5 PM tomorrow. See you then. Best, Paul."

Amber quickly replied, "Can't wait to hear the good news. See you at five. Fondly, Amber." Amber analyzed her use of the word "fondly." It didn't quite mean love, but it meant that she liked him more than closing with "sincerely" would convey.

❄ ❄ ❄

When Paul arrived for their date, he gathered Amber into his arms and hugged her snugly. "I've missed you so much."

"Me too," she responded. Shaking her head she said, "I mean, I've missed *you* very much too."

"I can't wait until the end of our date; may I kiss you now?"

"I think I'd like that," Amber said shyly.

He smiled as he leaned in toward Amber. When he kissed her, she felt like she had come home. His kiss was tender, sweet, and heartfelt—all the things she treasured in this man. When they parted, they gazed at each other for a few quiet moments.

"I could get used to this quickly," Paul said. "You look beautiful."

Amber's cheeks warmed at his complimentary words, and she nodded in understanding.

"Let's go have some fun." He locked her front door before handing the keys back to her as they started toward his truck.

"I haven't heard any live music for ages," Amber said. "I've been looking forward to this evening all week. Well, to be truthful, I've mostly been looking forward to spending some time with you."

"Do you know I've never heard you say the wrong thing to anyone in any situation, Amber? That must be a gift—that you instinctively know how to convey your love and optimism to people through your words."

"I thank God every day for bestowing that gift upon me. It really helps in my chosen career."

"I can imagine. By the way, have you always wanted to be a teacher?"

Amber laughed lightly before answering. "My little sisters and their friends used to come into my bedroom to play school. This was when I was in second or third grade and they were preschoolers and kindergartners. The girls sat at the small round table I used when I played house with my dolls and gave tea parties. I gave them paper and crayons to use for their schoolwork. Is this boring?"

Paul grinned. "No, I enjoy hearing about your life; I'll tell you if I get bored."

"I used to stand up in front of the girls and pretend my dresser was my teacher's desk. My parents set up a chalkboard on an easel for us to use for writing and drawing, so I'd use that to teach them spelling words and simple math problems. When they grew tired of schoolwork, I'd read storybooks. The girls loved to be read to and begged for the same stories over and over again, just like my first graders do now."

"Sounds like you got some great practice teaching from the time you were a kid."

"It was fun for all of us. My dream was to be a teacher when I grew up."

"I guess we can say you're living the dream," Paul teased, and they both laughed.

"I have great news about Tim and Barbara. They're thrilled that we want to have the fund-raiser to help out with the medical bills. Tim told me they've been wondering how they were going to make it through all of this financially. He said that he and Barbara have been at their wits' end trying to figure out a solution."

Amber clapped her hands together. "I just love it when a plan comes together!"

"They also think that it's a good idea to have the festival on Mary Noel's birthday. They believe that our plan may be just the thing to help their daughter snap out of her depression. To quote Tim, 'What six-year-old girl doesn't love being the center of attention on her birthday?' From what I know of little kids, I have to agree with him."

Amber chuckled. "You're both right about the attention thing. Now that we have the Simmons's blessing, we can move forward with confidence and really begin putting this thing together. What should we do first?"

"I think we should talk to Pastor Harris and ask him to make an announcement tomorrow during the church service and see if we can inspire some enthusiasm to get other community members to help us with the organizing and setup for the event."

"I'll get to church early tomorrow to speak to him," Amber volunteered.

"How about if I pick you up for church thirty minutes before the service, and we'll speak to him together?"

"I'd appreciate the backup. Next, I think we should set up committees for the various tasks that need to be accomplished: advertising, ticket sales, setup/cleanup, and vendor relations, to name a few. People who volunteer to help out can sign up for whatever committee they wish to serve on, and then we can really get things moving."

Paul reached across the seat to clasp Amber's hand and said, "You're absolutely amazing. I can call you Triple A from now on. Absolutely Amazing Amber."

Amber giggled before saying, "That's definitely a unique nickname."

"And appropriate for you." He smiled easily at her and squeezed her hand affectionately.

❄ ❄ ❄

The evening moved on swiftly, and before long it was approaching eleven o'clock. As the couple drove back to Apple Blossom, Paul asked Amber, "What was your favorite part of the evening? Eating? Listening to music? Talking?"

Without hesitation, she said, "Spending time with you."

Paul froze as her words sunk into his psyche. He flipped on his turn signal and coasted onto the shoulder of the road, far away from the other traffic. After parking safely, he turned off the engine and turned toward the woman sitting next to him. His voice became serious, his gaze intense. "Amber, listen, I want to say something to you."

"I'm sorry if I was too forward with what I just said," Amber jumped in. "You're not going to tell me you don't want to see me again, are you? If so, just get it over with and let me off easy. I've had so many guys make up stupid excuses about why they don't want to date me. It'll be easier on the both of us if you just say it straight out. Please."

If Amber hadn't looked so grief-stricken and stressed already, Paul would have laughed out loud at her sullen monologue. Realizing he must choose his words with great care, Paul paused before speaking. He reached out and took Amber's hands into his own.

"Amber Kellen, breaking things off with you is positively the last thing on my mind. What I originally intended to say was that I think I'm falling in love with you."

A hush fell over Amber as she absorbed what Paul had just said. Tears threatened to spill from her eyes, and when they did, Paul used his handkerchief to gently wipe them away.

"I'm not sure about the protocol for these types of situations. Frankly, I've never felt anything even close to what I feel for you. I've never been in love before."

Amber looked down at her lap as she confessed in a whisper, "No man's ever told me he was falling in love with me before. I've never been through this before either."

Tenderly raising her chin with his hand, Paul asked, "Does this mean you have feelings for me too?"

Amber smiled warmly at Paul. "Oh, I definitely have feelings for you, Paul. Loads and loads of *good* feelings. You might even classify them as 'I'm crazy about you' feelings."

"That's good to hear," he said, smiling. "The second thing I wanted to tell you, or maybe I should ask you, is that I'd like us to commit to dating each other exclusively."

"Are you asking me to go steady with you, Mr. Paul Sampson Watkins?" Amber asked.

"Yes. That's exactly what I'm asking," Paul replied seriously.

"Okay."

"Okay, what?"

"Okay, yes, I would absolutely love to date you exclusively."

At his gentle urging, Amber fell into Paul's arms, and they kissed earnestly for a few moments.

Leaning back into the driver's seat and starting the ignition, Paul said jokingly, "Now that that issue is settled, let's get you home so we can get up early for church tomorrow." They drove the rest of the way to Amber's apartment holding hands.

As the couple said one final, bittersweet good night on Amber's porch, they took a moment to pray together for God's wisdom and guidance in their relationship.

"Sweet dreams," Paul said, touching her nose with his fingertip.

"Sleep tight, Paul."

❄ ❄ ❄

At church the next morning, Amber and Paul spoke privately with Pastor Harris before he became occupied with preparations for the worship service.

"I'm certain many in this church family will be willing to help out with this festival for our little Mary Noel. I'll be glad to make an announcement this morning. Maybe you should be available here in the courtyard after the service to take a list of names and contact numbers so you can seriously begin organizing and planning. December twenty-fourth isn't that far off, you know."

"What a great idea, Pastor. Thank you for your enthusiasm and willingness to help us with some PR this morning."

"I'm always glad to help someone in need, and it sounds as if the Simmonses and little Mary Noel could use some good old-fashioned encouragement and support from their spiritual family."

True to his word, the church leader enthusiastically spoke about the festival and the need for the church family's support and intervention in the Simmons family's situation. After the service, Amber and Paul were happy to see that nearly two dozen families were interested in helping out.

Pete Wrightmann, a local farmer, was the first to talk with Amber and Paul. "My grandfather's antique sleigh has been restored, and I would be glad to offer rides to people that day. I have two snow white horses to pull the sleigh, and in addition to me, the sleigh can hold five or six other riders. We could charge ten dollars per family, and I'll contribute every cent I bring in to the medical expenses fund," he said.

"Also, do you want to hold the festival on my farm? My wife and I would be honored to host the event for you. We get a nice amount of snow there in our pasture every year. We even have some gentle hills we could use for the sledding and snowshoeing."

"Oh, what a blessing, Pete! We accept your offer." Amber's delight shone on her face and in her voice.

"Thanks, Pete. If you'll just write out your name and contact information, we'll be in touch." Paul shook hands with the genial farmer.

"I'd be glad to host a cookie-baking party in my professional kitchen at home," offered Cinda Erickson. "We could get a lot accomplished in one afternoon if I had half a dozen adult helpers. I'll donate all the ingredients since I can get everything at wholesale. We'll sell everything at a profit to contribute to the medical expenses fund."

"Thank you, Cinda. I'll contact you soon with details," Amber promised.

Next, the two brothers who owned a local sporting goods supply shop, Neal and Ned Allen, offered to loan them as many snowshoes and sleds as they needed for the festival's planned activities. "We'll drop them off and pick them up on whatever day and time you need," Neal offered.

"You guys are amazing." Paul shook each brother's hand enthusiastically.

A few moments later, the owners of the local coffee shop, Russ and Sherry Black, came by to volunteer to haul their portable chuck wagon out to the festival. They committed to serve hot chocolate, hot coffee, hot apple cider, and hot tea to the festival-goers. The Blacks wanted to donate all of the ingredients and supplies for their booth as well. Any profits would be donated directly to the medical expenses fund.

"Unbelievable! Thank you for your generosity," Paul said.

Amber and Paul found the outpouring of goodwill from their fellow citizens and congregants of the church to be very encouraging.

"This is amazing!" Amber said as Paul squeezed her shoulders affectionately.

As they were preparing to leave the courtyard, George Williams, owner of the local pizza parlor, approached them. "Hey, you two. I was just speaking with Russ and Sherry about the festival. I'd be more than happy to bring my pizza van over and serve hot pizza slices at the festival. I can't donate my entire receipts to you because my costs are high and business isn't so great right now. How about if I donate seventy-five percent of the receipts to the medical expenses fund? That way I can cover my food costs and still contribute to the cause."

"We accept! Thank you," Amber said.

"I'll bring along some hot sandwiches too, for those who don't like pizza. Although why anyone would pass up a huge slice of pipin' hot George Williams's original pizza is beyond me!"

The trio laughed together as George wrote down his contact information. Paul embraced Amber as if it were the natural thing to do and soon noticed she was weeping.

"What's wrong?" Paul asked quietly.

"Nothing's wrong. Everything's right! We're going to be able to really make a difference for the Simmonses."

"Since I have little background experience in the realm of understanding women, can you give me a clue here?" Then a look of understanding slowly spread across Paul's face. "Oh, I get it. Sometimes tears aren't shed because of sadness or grief; they can be shed in times of joy and happiness."

"You're a quick study." Amber smiled at him and kissed his cheek.

❄ ❄ ❄

"I hope the snow festival serves its purpose. I'm feeling more and more negative the longer this situation continues to drag on with Mary Noel," Paul confided one evening after their hospital visit.

"I understand. I keep reminding myself that I must trust the Lord and have faith that things will work out for Mary Noel. We need a miracle."

"I know, but it's been nearly three weeks since the accident. When are we going to see this miracle? I'm so downhearted about the whole thing. I'm really worried about Tim too. He looks awful. He never smiles or speaks in a positive tone anymore. He's lost so much weight that his clothes just hang on his already wiry frame."

"We just have to be patient and accept that there's only so much we can do to help out."

❄ ❄ ❄

One evening Amber's cell phone rang as she worked on her lesson plans at her kitchen table. Although she didn't recognize the phone number displayed on the screen, Amber answered anyway. "Hello?"

"Hi. Is this Amber?"

"Yes."

"Hi, Amber. My name is Ira Mayer. I live over in Moose Hill. Listen, I got your name and number from Russ at the Country Coffee Café. He was telling me about your fund-raiser for the Simmonses, and we'd like to help you out."

"Okay."

"My wife and I own a silk-screening shop, and I'd like to make sweatshirts for people to buy. I'd have to charge you my cost for the shirts, but I won't charge you for labor or delivery. You can set the price, and I'll donate everything above my costs to the medical expenses fund. How does that sound?"

"You're a godsend, Ira. Thank you so much." Amber couldn't wait to tell Paul about this new development.

"Russ told me the festival is called 'Angels for Mary Noel.' My wife, Michelle, is our graphic artist. How about I have her work up a couple of different designs for you to choose from? Once that's done, you can begin taking orders, and we'll have the shirts delivered in plenty of time for people to pick them up before the day of the festival."

"Excellent thinking. Just call me when the samples are ready, and I'll drive over to Moose Hill to see them."

"What color do you want the sweatshirts to be? Red or green?"

"I was thinking a pretty sky blue. That's Mary Noel's favorite color."

"Sky blue it is, then. Hey, thanks for letting us help out in this way. When our daughter, Haley, was little, she had to spend a lot of time in the hospital with her asthma, and the folks over in Apple Blossom were really supportive and encouraging to our family. We've never forgotten their kindness to us in our times of need."

"Thank *you,* Ira. Give your wife my best."

"I'll be in touch in a couple of days."

❄ ❄ ❄

Knowing that Paul was busy working on the festival's special projects that evening, Amber typed in a long text message and sent it to him. Within a few minutes, her cell phone chimed. Paul's text message read, "Amazing. Who would've thunk it? I know— it's a faith thing, huh? Love, Paul."

"Love? He signed off with the word 'love'? If he can text it, so can I." She composed a brief reply to Paul's message and sent it, including the "L" word in her closing.

A few moments later, her phone rang and Paul's name and number flashed on the screen. "Hello," Amber answered as she attempted to sound in control of her swirling emotions.

"Love," Paul said simply in his silky smooth voice. "You typed 'love' at the end of your message."

"That's correct."

"Does this mean—?"

"You tell me, Paul. You texted the 'L' word to me first."

He chuckled warmly and said, "Yeah, I guess I did. I know what I meant when I wrote it. I meant exactly what I wrote—'love.' I love you, Amber."

"That's what I thought. I meant the same when I sent my text to you just now."

"Man, I wish I was there with you right now so I could see your face when you said those three little magical words to me."

Amber giggled lightly and said, "I promise I'll tell you in person the next time I see you."

"Deal. Bye for now." Paul disconnected the call

before Amber even had a chance to respond.

"Okay, be like that, Mr. Watkins." She set her phone down and resumed trying to work on her lesson plans for the next week. Her mind kept wandering back to visions of Paul's handsome face and thoughts of their treasured time spent together. After a few fruitless minutes, Amber closed her lesson plan book and teacher's manual.

She picked up an historical romance novella she'd borrowed from the public library. She was quickly drawn into the story about a young school teacher trying to make a life for herself as a school marm in a one-room schoolhouse in the wild frontier of Montana in the late nineteenth century. The heroine was lonesome for now, but Amber knew once a handsome hero appeared on the scene, things would improve greatly for the lovely "Miss Madeline Amelia Hutchins."

❄ ❄ ❄

About fifteen minutes later, Amber heard a vehicle approach the apartment building. A door slammed loudly, and Amber heard a man's footsteps swiftly walking on the sidewalk. A gentle, insistent knock upon her front door startled Amber. As was her habit, she looked through the peephole before opening her door. She was relieved when she saw Paul's pleasant face smiling back at her.

The moment Amber opened the door, Paul stepped inside and closed the door behind him. "Hi there, gorgeous," he said as he ran his fingers through Amber's silken hair.

"Hi. This is certainly a nice surprise. I wasn't expecting to see you until the weekend," Amber said as she leaned into his hug.

"Well, I'm here."

"I noticed."

"You made me a promise when we were talking on the phone a few minutes ago."

"I seem to remember that, yes." Amber's eyes danced with mischief.

"Don't make me beg, Amber."

"I'll never make you beg." More seriously now, Amber said softly, "I love you, Paul Sampson Watkins." Amber's voice quivered a bit with emotion.

"I feel like the most fortunate man in the world right now." Paul kissed Amber until she was breathless. "I love you too." Paul's voice was husky with devotion.

The pair held each other for a few silent moments and then moved apart to look into each other's eyes.

"I've never told a man I loved him before," Amber said warily.

"And I've never said those magic words to a woman either," Paul said proudly. "Now I know what all the fuss is about with the guys at work when they fall in love. I feel like shouting out to the whole world that I'm in love with the most wonderful woman in the world!"

Amber smiled at this man who had captured her heart for the first and only time in her life. "Now I understand what those inspirational romance novels I've been reading since I was a teenager are talking about."

As he gazed intently into Amber's glistening eyes, he said seriously, "Amber, I want us to each pray about our relationship. This is too important, and I don't want to mess it up, all right?"

Amber nodded her acquiescence to his suggestion. "Isn't love grand?"

"It's absolutely wonderful."

CHAPTER SIX

Ira and Michelle Mayer had created three design proposals for the festival sweatshirts. Amber and Paul reviewed each one meticulously and agreed that the sweatshirt adorned with the white angel silhouette was definitely their first choice. Amber felt the whimsical design captured Mary Noel's affection for angels without being too childish. The simple slogan, "Angels for Mary Noel," was printed in navy blue ink with two words above and two words below the angel.

Dozens of sweatshirts had been ordered and would be delivered in boxes according to size to Amber's classroom. Sweatshirt orders had poured in from infant sizes all the way up to triple extra-large for some of the bigger and taller members of the community. Surprisingly, the surrounding communities got into the spirit of the festival and also ordered sweatshirts. The Mayers worked around the clock for a week to complete the orders.

The shirts were delivered the week of the festival, and an email was sent to those individuals and families who had placed orders. People dropped by Amber's classroom after school each day to pick up their orders. Amber was heartened to notice that not one family came to pick up their sweatshirts without asking if there was anything more they could do to help out with the festival. She'd never lived in a small, close-knit community before, and it was refreshing to learn how everyone contributed to helping a family in need.

The children in Amber's class had formed a little choir of sorts and were diligently practicing their two songs for Mary Noel under the competent tutelage of the school's music teacher, Mrs. Nichols. The ultra-talented Kathleen Nichols voluntarily worked with the children for thirty minutes after school each day. The children were memorizing the words to "Angels We Have Heard on High" and "Hark the Herald Angels Sing," and, with daily practice, were becoming fluent and poised in their presentation.

Amber practiced the words of the songs with her class as part of their daily recitation lesson, and the parents loyally worked on practicing the lyrics with their child each night. Mrs. Nichols worked on choral skills, tone, and pitch. Amber watched the children blossom in their knowledge of the songs and their presentation skills. She was certain their performance at the festival would have a huge positive impact on Mary Noel.

"Miss Kellen, do you think Mary Noel will like our choir?" Janae asked one day when the other children were outside at recess.

"I think she'll love it," Amber answered with a smile. "What do you think?"

"We want Mary Noel to feel better and come back to school real fast. Even the boys miss her. My daddy says most boys don't like girls when they're little. But the boys in our class like Mary Noel." Janae smiled a toothless grin at her teacher. Then she lowered her head and, more serious now, said, "I really miss my best friend. The hospital people won't even let me see her 'cuz I'm too little for vistin' hours. Mommy says hospitals think little kids are too noisy to be in there with sick people."

Amber's lips curled into a smile. "There are rules at the hospital just like we have rules here at school. Let's hope that Mary Noel does feel better and is able to come back to class after Christmas vacation. We just have to be patient."

"I know what patient means. It's a person who goes to see the doctor."

"That's true, but it also means to wait for something calmly. You know, without getting mad or upset."

Janae thought in puzzlement. "Oh, I get it. I think."

"All you need to understand right now is that Mary Noel is your friend, and she'll be glad that you and the other children sang two angel songs for her at the festival."

"Goodie! Bye, teacher!" Janae stuffed her arms into the sleeves of her hot pink parka and skipped out to the playground.

Amber smiled inwardly as she was once again reminded why she'd become a teacher. *I'm fortunate to be given the opportunity to shape young minds, even if this isn't always the easiest job in the world.*

❄ ❄ ❄

Paul and his crew were busy finishing the wooden angel cutouts and other wooden elements for the festival and would be installing them on the Wrightmanns' farm on Thursday night. He was more than pleased with the quality of the projects the crew had designed and built. The angel cutouts were embellished with a multitude of white twinkling lights. Everyone agreed that the lights made the perfect finishing touch for the festival's setting.

The ticket booth had a wood shingle roof with a slight overhang that made it perfect for any type of weather. Some of the carpenters helping out with the construction suggested the ticket booth could be used at future sporting events and community gatherings in Apple Blossom.

Dillon Silveira and Matthew Morgenstern from the high school construction academy called out to Paul. "Hey, Paul, can you come look at this?"

Paul strode over to where the two teens were working on completing the stage for the choir. The stage had a safety railing around all edges, just in case. As he approached the structure, Paul noticed several wooden cutouts leaning up against the front railing of the stage at regular intervals across the stage's width. He smiled as he realized the teens had created a birthday cake with seven candles along with several angels in varying poses to decorate the stage.

"Guys, this looks fantastic!"

"Thanks. They're not finished yet," Dillon said.

"Our girlfriends are both artists who work on the scenery for the theater arts department's performances, and they're going to come over tomorrow after school to paint these cutouts so they'll look really cool for the festival on Saturday," Matthew explained.

"They made the drawings for the cutouts and gave them to us to cut out in woodshop," Dillon added.

"The girls are going to make one of the angels look just like Mary Noel. We told them her hair color and that sky blue is her favorite color and everything." Matthew grinned.

"How will you mount the cutouts onto the stage?" Paul asked.

"We attached large O-rings to the stage railing and an S-hook to the back of each cutout. When the festival's over for the day, we'll unhook these and give them to the Simmonses to take home to decorate their yard for Christmas," Dillon smiled broadly.

"You two are really something. You have some natural talent for carpentry too. Thanks for all you've done to make this event even more special for the Simmons family." Paul shook hands with both of the teens. "I can't wait to see what—who are your girlfriends?"

"Chelsea and Marie. Trust me; they are the nicest, prettiest, most-talented girls in the whole school. They're best friends just like me and Dillon," Matthew chimed in proudly.

"I believe it. I can't wait to see how Chelsea and Marie decorate your handiwork. Thanks a million, guys." As the boys walked away, Paul shook his head in amazement. "My previous slightly negative impression of teenage boys has just been wiped away," Paul said to no one in particular.

Rubbing his beard absentmindedly as he looked around at the Wrightmanns' now crowded pasture, Paul realized that the projects he'd ultimately been responsible for designing and building were of the highest quality. Experienced carpenters and construction workers from Apple Blossom and the surrounding communities had made an important contribution to the success of the festival. Paul had been amazed with the generosity of the local lumber yards and building supply houses.

The setup looked better than Paul had ever imagined. Amber would be so thrilled when she arrived on Saturday morning. More important, though, Paul hoped that Tim and Barbara and Mary Noel would be cheered up by the community's efforts in their behalf.

❄ ❄ ❄

Thoughts of the Simmons family's situation occupied Paul's mind throughout his days and nights no matter his task. Mary Noel was still in the hospital, although she was responding slightly to her parents and teacher at unpredictable intervals. She was definitely not the talkative, inquisitive little girl that everyone knew and loved. She continued to be moody and depressed the majority of the time, but the doctors had given their permission for the patient to ride with her parents in the horse-drawn sleigh at the festival. Her leg and arm were still in casts, but the patient was no longer in physical pain. Her physicians conferred and told the girl's parents that the outing would greatly benefit the youngster.

Amber made confirmation calls to all of the vendors and people who had volunteered to help with the parking, setup, cleanup, and so forth. Everyone was eagerly anticipating the event. Best of all, the little town of Apple Blossom had been graced with twenty-eight inches of fresh snow, frigid temperatures, and clear jewel-tone blue skies. Amber and Paul were delighted but remained cautiously optimistic about the turnout for the event.

"We'll know by Saturday night whether our efforts have paid off," Paul said Wednesday evening over dinner at Amber's apartment. It was the first time she had cooked a meal for him. After having restaurant food, frozen dinners, and canned goods for most of his meals, Paul told Amber he was enjoying the succulent homemade pot roast with potatoes and carrots that she had prepared.

"I don't know how you managed it after working all day, but this dinner is really delicious."

"Thanks. It's the wonder of a slow cooker," she teased.

"A slow cooker?"

"Yes, you throw everything into it in the morning, and the meal is ready to be served when you get home."

"Sounds simple. Maybe I need to get one of those. I'm so tired of eating canned chili, scrambled eggs, and frozen entrees for dinner. Are there any last minute details about the festival we need to go over tonight?"

"No, I don't think so. Everything seems to be going smoothly because we have a great community that's pulling together," Amber sighed. "We've been blessed with all of the merchants who have dedicated their time and talents along with the other people who are buying sweatshirts and tickets. I'm so glad to be a part of this whole thing."

"Me too," Paul said quietly. "Hey, did I tell you that the local lumber yards and building supply houses have agreed to pitch in and give us everything that we ordered for the wooden structures free of charge?"

"That's generous. Sounds like I'll have a lot of handwritten thank you notes to send out after the holidays."

"Yeah, we used a lot of lumber for the stage and those angel cutouts. I'm sure we're going to make our goal on the funds for the medical bills."

"I made some brownies for dessert. From scratch—not from a box—just so you know. Would you like one smothered with vanilla ice cream? I heard from Hazel that's your all-time favorite dessert."

"That sounds delicious. The words 'from scratch' are music to a bachelor's ears." Paul watched Amber as she moved around the kitchen with ease, plating the dessert she'd made especially for him.

"Thanks," Paul said when Amber placed a generous helping of the sweet treat in front of him. Paul noticed she didn't serve any dessert to herself. "Where's your dessert?"

"Oh, I'm skipping dessert tonight. I need to go to

bed early, and I can't sleep if I eat too late in the evening." Suddenly Amber lowered her eyes as if embarrassed. "Was that too much information?"

"Nope. Do what you have to do to take care of
yourself." Paul dug his spoon into his brownie with
gusto and smiled with satisfaction when his taste buds
soaked up the chocolate flavoring that he loved above
all other treats. "De-licious!" he declared enthusiastically, causing Amber to laugh aloud.

"I'm really getting excited about Saturday, but I'll
admit I'm tired. I haven't felt this exhausted since my
final year of the teaching credential program in college when I was taking my graduate classes and student teaching full time. I was tired then too, but I *was*
a lot younger back then."

"Uh, excuse me, but didn't you just finish your
credential program six months ago?" Paul asked with
a distinct twinkle in his eyes.

Amber blushed pink before answering. "Yes.
Well, somehow it seemed like a lot longer ago than six
months." The melody of Amber's sweet giggle tickled Paul's soul. "You polished off that dessert faster
than anyone I've ever seen. Maybe we should put you
on one of those talent shows on TV."

"I have special talents you haven't yet discovered."
He carried his dishes to the sink and turned to ask,
"Want me to help with the dishes?" She waved him
off with the shake of her head.

"Well then, I think I'll say good-bye so that we can both get some rest. Tomorrow night I'll be at the farm setting up the angel cutouts and other staging elements. Can I see you on Friday night?"

"I'd enjoy that." Amber batted her eyelashes in Paul's direction.

"I will too," he replied before pulling Amber into his embrace. "Thank you for the delicious dinner. I didn't know you were so handy in the kitchen."

"There's a lot you don't know about me."

"Do tell," Paul joked.

"No, you'll have to wait and discover things about me as time unfolds."

"Okay, it's a deal. Love you."

"I love you too."

❄ ❄ ❄

On Friday night Paul took Amber to George's pizza parlor for a light dinner. During their meal, people stopped by to offer words of encouragement about the festival the next day. Many expressed their excitement about the event. Several parents of young children mentioned that their little ones were looking forward to the snow activities and contests and singing in the choir.

George personally delivered their order to the table. He babbled on good-naturedly about his pizza cart and the pizzas and sandwiches he would be selling. "I hope I sell out of everything I prep. If I do, I'll be able to make a hefty donation for the cause. I'll see you two lovebirds tomorrow, okay?"

"Lovebirds?" Paul raised his eyebrows as George scurried back to the kitchen.

"He means well," Amber said with a smile.

"Just think, tomorrow night at this time the festival will be over, and we'll know just how much, or how little, we helped the Simmonses."

"I just can't wait to see their faces when they see all that people have done for them," Amber responded dreamily. "I'm so excited!"

❄ ❄ ❄

Saturday morning dawned cold and clear. Amber ran to her kitchen window to check the weather before eating her breakfast. The deck attached to her living room was covered with a couple of inches of fresh snow. "Awesome!" she sang out exuberantly.

Her phone chimed, and Amber rushed over to read Paul's latest text, "Good morning! This is the day that the Lord hath made. Let us rejoice and be glad in it. ILU, PSW." As their relationship had progressed, the couple had taken to using some abbreviations in their text messages.

"It's going to be a fantastic day here in AB. See you soon. Love ya, ABK."

Amber moved quickly through her morning routine

of reading her bible, praying, stretching, and writing in her journal. She was anxious to get cleaned up and dressed so she'd be ready when Paul arrived at ten o'clock to pick her up. She had purchased a new light blue snowsuit and cozy white snow boots for the occasion. The vendors would begin arriving at Wrightmanns' farm at eleven o'clock to set up and share a potluck lunch before the big event officially launched at one o'clock.

By the time Paul arrived to pick her up, Amber felt at peace about the day's happenings, but she also felt an excitement that she'd never felt before. Seeing him was the highlight of the day for Amber and she told him so, earning herself a warm hug and tender kiss.

"Let's hit the trail, cowgirl," Paul said. Amber locked her front door, and they headed out to his truck.

"Cowgirl?" She wrinkled her nose in feigned distaste.

"Well, we're spending the day at a farm so I thought the moniker was appropriate."

"Moniker? Have you been playing with the thesaurus on your phone again?" Amber's laughter resonated throughout the truck's cab.

Paul abruptly quieted as if lost in his own deep thoughts. Amber sensed some discomfort in the way he stared out the truck's windshield. His jaw was set firmly in a way she'd not observed previously.

"Is everything all right?"

"Yeah, fine," he answered halfheartedly.

"I was just teasing about the thesaurus." She reached across the front seat to touch his forearm gently.

"Yeah, I know," Paul snapped.

"In California, cowgirls usually live on ranches, but I guess a cowgirl can also live on a farm. Do the Wrightmanns have cows?" She tickled his stomach as he buckled up the seat belt. "I can't wait to see your angel cutouts. You and your crew did double duty building those and setting up the rest of the staging areas at the Wrightmanns' farm. Thank you."

"You're welcome," he said gruffly.

"Paul?" Amber spoke hesitantly.

"Yes?"

"What's happened to your mood since we got in your truck? I mean, you seemed so cheerful and then all of the sudden—"

"Amber, I need to ask you something. It's something I've been wondering about with us."

Startled by the intense tone in his voice, she stilled and asked warily, "What is it?"

"Does it bother you that you're so much more educated than I am? I mean, I'm a high school graduate and all, but you have a bachelor's degree *and* a master's degree in education. Are we a good match or is it hard for you to know that you're more intelligent than I am?" Pain surrounded Paul's strained eyes and mouth as he looked to Amber for her honest response.

"First of all, who said I'm more intelligent than you? You're intelligent in ways I could never dream of being intelligent." She spoke gently, sensing this issue was of vital importance to him.

"Like what?"

"For instance, geometry was my most difficult subject in high school and college. I struggled and struggled and barely passed my courses. I even had tutoring and extra help from the teachers and professors. I absolutely couldn't grasp the spatial concepts involved in that type of math. Yet, you're a journeyman carpenter who puts geometric theories into practice every day with ease. And you're successful at it."

"I never thought about it that way."

"Second, I love and respect you for the man that you are, not what you know. You're compassionate, kind to a fault, generous with your time and talents, and witty and fun to be with too."

"Really?"

"Yes, really. You're also a good listener, and you're kinda cute in a masculine sort of way. You're also charming." Amber smiled. "Any other questions or concerns, cowboy?"

"I guess not. It was just my self-doubts coming to the surface. Thanks for the reassurance."

Leaning across the front seat, Amber planted her most sincere kiss on his weather-beaten cheek. "You're a great guy, and I'm so grateful you're in my life."

"Likewise," Paul answered before he cupped Amber's chin and kissed her deeply several times. "Let's get a move on, cowgirl."

Amber touched her fingers to her mouth; she didn't mind being called cowgirl all *that* much when her beau kissed her silly.

❊ ❊ ❊

As the couple rode to the Wrightmanns' farm for the festival, they chatted about the plans for the day. The earlier tension between them had dissipated much to Amber's relief. The pair was still getting to know each other, and they were discovering the strengths and weaknesses of the other through open, honest communication.

"Do you think our plan will work, Paul? I mean, do you think Mary Noel will snap out of her depression when she sees everyone and all the angels?"

"If you want my personal opinion, I think that this will turn out to be an extraordinary day in the little patient's life and in her parents' lives too." He squeezed Amber's hand in his as he carefully traversed the highway out to the farm.

"I hope you're right."

"Amber, you'll soon learn that I'm always right even when I'm wrong." The two laughed in harmony.

❊ ❊ ❊

The farm was a hub of activity when the couple

arrived. Most of the vendors had already arrived and were taking directions from Peter Wrightmann. The small ticket booth at the entrance of the farm that Paul and his crew had constructed was decorated with colorful steamers and white and blue balloons. It would be staffed with two ladies from the town's women's auxiliary. The food stands were already set up in a circle surrounding the huge angel cutouts. Several wooden picnic tables with long benches sat amongst the angels in the food area awaiting hungry festival attendees.

Paul took the enthusiastic and curious Amber on a tour of the grounds. She gasped when she saw the stage Paul's crew had built. It was set off to one side of the food area for the choir's performance.

"Look at the stage. It's adorable!"

Paul shook his head in disbelief when he saw how the stage had been painted completely white. Another of Dillon's and Matthew's finishing touches, he imagined. Not only that, the cutouts the boys had built had been skillfully painted by Marie and Chelsea. One of the little angels looked just like Mary Noel with blonde hair, blue eyes, and rosy cheeks. This angel was wearing a sky-blue dress and a pair of lovely silver wings. The girls had used silver glitter paint to stencil large snowflakes on the railings around the stage.

"Wow! Those kids really went all out on their art-work. I'm going to call their teachers and brag on them about their creativity and dedication to our cause."

"Mary Noel is going to love this," Amber said, clinging to Paul's arm. "Was decorating the stage your idea?"

"No, actually two teen boys from the high school designed and built it. They also made the cutouts following designs that their girlfriends thought up. The girlfriends painted the little cutouts. Look at the birthday cake cutout."

"Oh, it has seven candles on it with sprinkles and hearts and Mary Noel's name. They did such a fantastic job!"

The couple continued their tour, greeting other volunteers along the way. The snowman building contest, snowball toss, and snow angel areas were further down the road where the snow had formed deep drifts. Slightly further up the road where the terrain was hilly was the area set aside for the snowshoe races and sled rides. The Wrightmanns' splendorous antique, two-horse sleigh was standing next to the mounting steps Paul and his crew had built for that purpose. The three-seat sleigh had been freshly painted a cherry red with white trim. Snowball and Snowflake were likely still snug and warm in the sizeable stable, no doubt, enjoying an extra serving of oats for their trouble.

"Everything looks absolutely perfect! I can't wait to see the two snow white horses that'll pull the sleigh."

"Promise me you'll save a sleigh ride all alone with me before we head home later?"

"Yes, Mr. Watkins, I'll take a sleigh ride with you. Let's start setting up the tables for the potluck. I brought some plastic tablecloths and paper goods and utensils for everyone to use."

The couple worked efficiently to get the tables lined with tablecloths and set up for the vendors and other volunteers. Amber and Paul thought it would be fun for the vendors to have an opportunity to relax and have something to eat and drink before the festival attendees arrived. People began carrying over baskets, bowls, and pans of food to share. Soon Pastor Harris called everyone over and offered a blessing for the bounty they were about to share.

The conversation was lively and joyful, and the food disappeared quickly. People were obviously enjoying the camaraderie among the vendors and volunteers. Everyone pitched in to clean up and check over things one last time before the gates officially opened. With the ticket booth deftly staffed, the gates of the "Angels for Mary Noel Festival" officially opened early due to the sizeable line that was building up at the entrance to the grounds.

"Look how many people are here already!" Amber exclaimed. She hugged Paul snugly.

"I told you to have a little faith, didn't I?"

"Oh, you . . ."

"I'll go flick the light switches on the angels. They look really pretty when the lights twinkle."

"What should I do?" Amber asked.

"Supervise and greet our guests," Paul said. He planted a kiss on her chilled cheek and walked away.

By two o'clock the festival was packed. There were about four times as many people in attendance as the organizers had ever dreamed. The Simmonses were scheduled to arrive at three o'clock for their sleigh ride and the choir's performance, so Amber took a moment to wander around to see the various happenings and activities.

The sled and snowshoe races were popular with the boys and teens while the snow angel and snowman areas were heavily attended by girls and adults. Everyone enjoyed the snowball toss even when they were pelted with globs of wet snow. There was a long line for the sleigh ride with Mr. Wrightmann, but he assured every family they would get a turn before he took his extremely patient, pleasant horses back into their stable for the day.

❄ ❄ ❄

As it was approaching three o'clock, Amber went to search for Paul. She found him at the pizza booth enjoying a slice of George Williams's famous pepperoni and sausage pizza. "Hey, cowboy, it's almost time for the guest of honor to arrive."

"I'm ready," he murmured as he finished chewing his last bite of pizza. "De-licious, George. Thanks!"

"I'm guessing you didn't get enough to eat at the potluck earlier?" Amber asked.

"I'm a growing boy with two hollow legs. Haven't you learned that yet? Besides, I wanted to make a donation to the medical expenses fund." He playfully grabbed Amber's gloved hand and pulled her toward the entrance. "I want to be up front when Tim and his family arrive."

"Look, I think I see Tim carrying Mary Noel in from their car right now. There's Barbara too!"

Paul and Amber walked toward the Simmonses, who each smiled ear to ear. Mary Noel's face was more animated than Amber had seen since before the accident. She whispered to Paul, "Look. Mary Noel's eyes are shining with joy. This may just work after all."

He whispered in reply, "It'll work."

As the couple reached the guest of honor and her family, Paul gently took Mary Noel into his arms to give his friend a rest. "Hi, Mary Noel. It sure is great to see you looking so healthy today." Although the girl remained silent, her eyes danced with excitement.

"Looks like there's a huge turnout for this festival," Tim said.

"I can't believe how many people are present. You've really outdone yourselves on our account. Thank you so much." Barbara began to cry.

"No tears today. This is a festival, and we are all going to be 'festive' no matter what," Amber said.

"Spoken just like a first grade teacher. Thanks for the reminder," Barbara said as she hugged Amber warmly.

"Let's get Mary Noel up on the sleigh, and you can tour the grounds as a family. People will want to greet you and speak to you all," Paul said.

Young voices approached and were soon shouting, "Hi, Mary Noel!" "Happy birthday, Mary Noel!" "Merry Christmas, Mary Noel!" "Mary Noel, I missed you!" "Wait 'til you hear our songs!" "I like you, Mary Noel!"

Mary Noel responded with a brilliant smile directed at her classmates.

"Don't you want to talk to your friends?" Barbara asked her daughter patiently.

The girl replied with a dramatic shake of her head. When they reached the sleigh, Paul handed the girl up to Mr. Wrightmann, who carefully set her upon the backseat and covered her legs with a warm, colorful, handmade quilt. Mr. and Mrs. Simmons climbed up into the sleigh to join their mesmerized daughter.

"Mr. and Mrs. Simmons, my wife, Virginia, made that quilt especially for your Mary Noel in the hope that it would keep her warm and give her comfort inside and out. Happy birthday, Mary Noel, from the entire Wrightmann Family." He was rewarded with a shy smile from the birthday girl.

The quilt featured blocks of colorful pinwheels that virtually twirled with realistic vibrancy. A cute, hand-embroidered angel adorned the center block. The backing on the quilt was made of soft, sky blue flannel with a snowflake print on it. The edges of the quilt were finished with lilac binding.

Barbara broke the silence, excitement laced through her voice. "Look at this cute quilt, everyone. These colors are my daughter's favorites, Mr. Wrightmann. Pinks, blues, and purples. How did your wife know?"

"Miss Kellen may have helped out Virginia with the color and fabric selection just a bit," the kind farmer replied.

"Thank you, Amber. This quilt is a real treasure," Tim said.

"Look, everyone! There's a sweet little angel and pinwheels. And look, here's your name, Mary Noel." Barbara's voice was filled with wonder and emotion.

Mary Noel's tiny fingertips carefully traced the threads Mrs. Wrightmann had so lovingly stitched to make the letters of her name and the outline of the angel appear on the fabric. The girl quickly realized this was her very own special quilt. The youngster beamed in gratitude at Mr. Wrightmann before bestowing glowing smiles on her parents and lastly Amber and Paul.

"Mr. Wrightmann, we'd like to personally thank your wife for this unbelievable gift. Could you introduce us to her back at the festival, please?" Tim's voice faltered with emotion.

"It'd be my pleasure, young man," the farmer replied with a grin.

❆ ❆ ❆

Paul helped Amber up into the sleigh and then climbed in and sat next to her on the middle seat directly behind Mr. Wrightmann. When the driver had checked that everyone was settled, he quietly said, "Here we go." Then with a click of his tongue and a firm, "Giddy-up," he signaled the horses to begin walking. The magnificent snow white horses, the honorable Snowball and Snowflake, began pulling the sleigh smoothly and surely.

Paul leaned close to Amber and whispered into her ear so only she could hear him. "Remember, you promised me a ride later with just the two of us."

"I remember all of my promises," she replied with a smile.

Mr. Wrightmann took the group to view all of the different activities, including making a loop around his house where a bountifully decorated fresh Christmas tree stood proudly in the front window. All too soon Snowball and Snowflake were heading back to the small stage where the children's choir was waiting to perform.

❆ ❆ ❆

As the horses pulled up in front of the stage, Janae began jumping up and down and waving at Mary Noel. "Mary Noel! Mary Noel! Hi! Remember me? I'm your best friend, Janae Montanez. Hi, Mary Noel! Happy birthday!" A quiet chuckle rumbled through the crowd of onlookers. Janae was not at all shy about sharing her joy at seeing her best friend again.

The children in the choir each wore an official festival sweatshirt. The light blue sweatshirts mirrored the brilliant winter sky above. The choir sang their two rehearsed angel songs perfectly before sharing a raucous rendition of the "Happy Birthday" song customized with the birthday girl's name. After receiving a loud ovation from the onlookers, the youngsters clambered down the stage stairs to the ground and surrounded the sleigh. Mr. Wrightmann reminded the children to stay back from the horses and to remain quiet and still so they wouldn't scare the sometimes skittish animals.

As was to be expected, Janae took the lead by pointing to the huge lighted angel cutouts standing a few feet away. In a loud whisper, the girl exclaimed, "Look! Angels! They're angels for Mary Noel!"

"I love angels, Janae."

No one recognized the small voice that spoke at first. Amber turned around and casually asked, "Did you say something?"

"I said I love angels, Miss Kellen. Today's my birthday, teacher. I'm seven now."

"Seems I heard something about today being your birthday. Happy birthday!" Amber smiled warmly at her student and patted her affectionately on the knee.

"Thank you, God," Tim said tearfully.

"It's a miracle," his wife announced shakily.

"We're all glad to hear that you like angels. Oh, and happy birthday," Paul said.

"Thank you, Mr. Paul. You're always so nice to me." Mary Noel smiled at the stunned carpenter.

"How about some hot chocolate and an angel cookie, birthday girl?" Pastor Harris asked as he looked on from the snowy ground below.

"I love angel cookies," she replied enthusiastically. The birthday girl devoured the sugar cookie and a cup of hot chocolate in record time before resuming chattering cheerfully to her family and friends for the next fifty minutes.

"Wait till the doctors hear about this," Tim said to Paul as the young father shook his head in awe.

"Seems like the plan worked. This looks like a real Christmas miracle to me," Paul said quietly to the other adults.

"I think I've witnessed two miracles here today," Amber said. "The healing of a little girl who could no longer fight the power of love and kindness, and the miracle of a community pulling together to make a positive difference in the lives of their neighbors."

"Well said, Miss Kellen," Paul said proudly.

"Thank you both from the bottom of our hearts for all you and everyone else did to make today happen." Tim shook Paul's hand firmly and then hugged Amber warmly.

"You're very welcome," the young couple spoke in unison.

"We're heading home. We've had an exhausting few weeks. I'll call the doctor and tell him what's happened this afternoon. I hope he'll release Mary Noel from the hospital for Christmas Day tomorrow." Barbara sounded relieved, yet exhilarated, as she shared this welcome news.

"Time to go home, little one," Tim said, gathering his daughter into his arms.

"I can't wait to go home to our house, Daddy. Will Santa come to our house tonight?"

"We'll just have to wait and see, now won't we?" came her mother's response as she winked at Amber and Paul behind Mary Noel's back.

❄ ❄ ❄

Paul rushed ahead of Amber as she headed back to the festival grounds. When she rounded the corner near the ticket booth, she saw him waiting patiently at the bottom of the steps used for boarding the sleigh.

Snowflake and Snowball stood at attention, and Mr. Wrightmann wore a smile that hinted that he knew what Paul was up to and he approved heartily!

Amber enjoyed her second sleigh ride even more than the first. Both men pointed out interesting highlights of the grounds that she hadn't noticed on her earlier ride. When they arrived at the window hosting the Wrightmanns' Christmas tree, the driver urged the horses to pause. "I thought you might like to have a close-up look at the decorations my wife made for our tree," the farmer said.

"It really is a gorgeous tree, Mr. Wrightmann. Thank you for sharing it with us," Amber responded.

Leaning her head close to Paul's, Amber whispered, "I hope to one day have a lovely Christmas tree to display in a big picture window in my home. A beautiful tree makes the whole scene so festive and inviting." With a contented sigh, she hugged Paul tightly before kissing him tenderly.

"Giddy-up," Mr. Wrightmann said once again to Snowball and Snowflake as the sleigh continued on its loop back to the festival grounds.

CHAPTER SEVEN

*L*ater on Amber and Paul were sitting in front of her fireplace resting for a while before heading to church for the Christmas Eve service. She turned toward Paul and spoke softly, "I'm still shocked that we earned close to ten thousand dollars for the medical expenses. Are you surprised?"

"No, not really."

"You're not even a little bit surprised about the amount of money we collected?"

"Well, I'll admit I had my sights set on raising a couple or maybe three thousand dollars. People were very generous, from the vendors to the volunteers to the attendees."

"Yes, they were. Apple Blossom really caught the Christmas spirit this year."

"So did I." Paul hugged Amber close and kissed her on the cheek.

"Let's go to church. I've always loved the candle-light Christmas Eve service."

❄ ❄ ❄

The Christmas Eve service at the historic country church was a truly joyous and awe-inspiring occasion. The sanctuary was decorated with evergreen garlands, swags, and wreaths, each embellished with a large crisp red satin bow. A lit Christmas tree adorned with various styles of angel and star ornaments—all handmade lovingly by members of the congregation—stood in the narthex of the church. A large, antique, carved-wood nativity scene sat atop a handmade wool quilt covering the table in the center of the altar area. Red candles flickered in their massive brass holders positioned on either side of the altar. The mood was set for an enriching evening of worship by the attendees of the little country church.

Pastor Harris began with an announcement chronicling the success of the fund-raiser held to benefit the Simmonses. "Thanks to your outpouring of love and monetary support this afternoon, God created two miracles in the lives of this deserving family. First of all, Mary Noel began communicating with those around her naturally for the first time since the accident four weeks ago. Second, I understand that the funds collected through this event far surpassed anyone's expectations. Well, anyone's expectations except God's." The congregation chuckled respectfully. "Therefore, I believe our first hymn will be sung with special meaning tonight. Please join me in the singing of 'Angels We Have Heard on High.'"

Paul and Amber rose with the congregation and sang an especially spirited rendition of the time-honored Christmas carol. A countenance of peace and serenity settled over the congregation as Pastor Harris read the story of Christ's birth from the Book of Luke. Paul reached for Amber's hand and held it firmly in his own as they experienced the majesty of arguably the most treasured story in the New Testament.

The children's choir sang "Away in a Manger" and "O, Little Town of Bethlehem" under the competent direction of Pastor Harris's talented wife, Gloria. A string quintet played "The First Noel" and "We Three Kings" accompanied by Mrs. Harris on the piano. Lastly, a soul-stirring rendition of "O Holy Night" was performed by the church's brilliant baritone, Jerald Leland. By the end of the service, the presence of the Christ child could be felt keenly in the midst of the congregation.

"That was so beautiful," Amber whispered to Paul through her tears. She was reassured of his agreement by the loving squeeze of his hand. As she raised her eyes to look at Paul, she noticed his eyes also glistened with tears.

He leaned in close to whisper in her ear. "I'm grateful to share this extraordinary evening with you."

❄ ❄ ❄

As was the tradition in the little country church, everyone over the age of ten was given a candle in a brass holder as they exited the sanctuary. The congregants stood in a large circle out on the church's courtyard, and Pastor Harris lit his candle. Then he turned to his left and to his right and lit the candles of those standing directly next to him. In turn, each person shared his flame with the person next to him until all of the candles were lit. It truly was a sight to behold.

At that moment, Mrs. Harris's clear soprano voice began singing the first verse of "Silent Night" a cappella. As the congregation joined in musical praise of the miracle of Jesus's birth, the atmosphere in the courtyard became one of worshipful reverence. The faces of young and old glowed in the flickering light, and Amber could tell that both she and Paul felt the power of God's love once again. Many faces were stained with tears of gratitude and hope.

"Let's bow our heads in prayer, my friends. Father, thank you for so unselfishly sending your greatest gift to earth two thousand years ago. We thank you for your unyielding presence, wisdom, and guidance in our lives. Bless each of us as we depart this place of worship to spend a festive time with our loved ones celebrating Jesus's birth. Amen."

❄ ❄ ❄

Darkness descended upon the courtyard as the flames were extinguished, and the candles were collected by the ushers. Momentarily the lampposts were illuminated so everyone could make their way to the parking lot and depart for the family Christmas traditions that awaited them at home. Cheerful shouts of "Merry Christmas, everyone!" rang out as families rushed to their cars.

Pastor Harris cornered Amber and Paul before they made it over to the parking lot. "Listen, you two. I want to thank you again for all you did to facilitate the Simmons family's miracles today. I truly hope this Christmas is a most special occasion for the both of you. Merry Christmas!"

"Merry Christmas, Pastor." Amber leaned in to shake his hand.

"I hope you and your family have a very Merry Christmas, sir." Paul pumped the pastor's hand briskly.

"I'll pray for you about those plans of yours, young man," Pastor Harris whispered to Paul as Amber turned to walk to the parking lot.

"I'd appreciate that; I need all the prayers I can get right about now, sir."

❄ ❄ ❄

Paul lingered on Amber's doorstep while he waited for her to unlock her front door. "I'll pick you up around ten o'clock tomorrow morning, if you'd like. That way we'll have a few minutes together before everyone meets at my house. I think you'll really get along fine with my dad. He's very excited to meet you."

"I'm looking forward to meeting him too."

"I just know Dad'll love you as much as I do. You're pretty special, you know?"

Amber giggled lightly. "That's what you always tell me. I'm looking forward to spending some long overdue time with my parents and sisters."

Amber's two younger sisters, Edie and Ivy, had flown to Vermont with their parents from Southern California earlier that evening. The foursome had driven to Apple Blossom to stay in the local bed and breakfast inn for several nights. Amber had offered to put all four of them up at her apartment. When she mentioned that her apartment was about six hundred square feet in size, everyone agreed the sleeping and bathroom arrangements would be a little tight there. It was the first time in the past few years the entire Kellen clan would be together on Christmas Day, and Amber was beside herself with anticipation at celebrating the holidays with her family.

"Mind if I check my phone to see if I heard from my family?"

"Help, yourself," Paul replied.

"Oh, my sisters sent me some text messages from the bed and breakfast inn while we were in church tonight. So far they just love Apple Blossom. Christmas Day has always been a special holiday in our household, so everyone's excited about tomorrow. I'm especially thrilled that it's the first Christmas you and I will spend together."

"Sweet dreams." Paul kissed Amber tenderly before opening the front door and watching her disappear inside. "I'm glad we could share the Christmas Eve service together tonight. Tomorrow will be a memorable Christmas for both of us, I suspect. I love you."

"Good night; I love you too—very much. Now you need to get home and get to sleep so Santa will visit." Amber giggled as she partially closed her front door against the cold winter air. She felt a tug on her heart as she watched Paul walk away from her apartment.

When he reached his truck, Paul turned to face Amber and said, "Merry Christmas!"

"Merry Christmas!"

❄ ❄ ❄

Santa probably won't be paying me a visit after all

because there is absolutely no way I'm going to be able to sleep tonight. Paul laughed aloud as he hopped into his truck and headed home to visit with his father briefly before retiring for the evening. He had a busy day ahead of him beginning early the next morning, and he wanted to try to get some well-deserved rest.

CHAPTER EIGHT

Christmas Day promised to be a joyous occasion for Amber and Paul for several reasons. First, it was a celebration of Christ's humble birth. It was also the first time their families would see them together as a couple. Amber's family had been invited by Paul to gather at his sizeable family home for a Christmas feast.

Paul's father had driven in from his apartment in New York City. Since his wife's death, Sam Watkins had been an infrequent visitor to Apple Blossom. Paul rarely had time to take off from his job to travel to New York City for a visit with his father, so it was an emotional and joyous reunion for both men.

Amber and her two younger sisters, Edie and Ivy, shrieked with unabashed joy when they were reunited. Her mother and father were genuinely happy to see their oldest daughter, whom they had missed every single day since she had moved to Vermont in August. Introductions were made, and everyone sat down in front of the Christmas tree to visit for a while before the kitchen preparations began.

Paul was a gracious host and treated Amber's younger sisters as he might his own. His conversation with Amber's parents was affable, and it appeared that the two family groups melded together in perfect harmony. The Kellen women cooked a small turkey and prepared several traditional side dishes for everyone's enjoyment. Paul and Sam provided handcrafted bread and rolls along with an assortment of pies custom-ordered from the local bakery shop. As the host, Paul was encouraged by the others to offer the blessing before carving the turkey.

Conversation at dinner was lively and varied. Paul, Sam Watkins, and Mr. Kellen talked business and sports while the ladies caught up on their news. The meal was delicious and well-received. Over hot tea and pie, each person shared a special Christmas memory. Some of the memories were silly and some were touching. A sense of friendship and camaraderie settled over the gathering. It was an extraordinary Christmas celebration. As expected, everyone ate too much and complained about it later.

❄ ❄ ❄

After dessert everyone gathered around Paul's stunning evergreen tree for a gift exchange. Amber and Paul had decorated the tree together one evening, embellishing it with twinkling white lights and ornaments of all shapes and sizes. Of course, an angel adorned the treetop, watching over everyone as a symbol of God's everlasting presence in their lives. Much laughter and teasing was shared as each gift was revealed. The recipients treasured the books, clothing, jewelry, CDs, DVDs, snow globes, and gift cards, and everyone had a good time.

After promising Paul and Amber that they would all work together to clean the kitchen thoroughly, their family dismissed them to "go have some fun together." Paul and Amber took his golden retriever, Dallas, for a walk through the woods surrounding the property. The couple deeply enjoyed their time together and were happy to escape the chaos of having so many of their family members bustling around the house.

"Peace at last." Paul sighed audibly and pulled Amber closer to him. She was tucked snugly under his arm. She was holding his waist and beaming up at him with a twinkle in her eyes. "You know what gift I'm most thankful for this Christmas?" Paul asked seriously.

"The slow cooker and cookbook set I gave you?" Amber's eyes danced with mischief.

"No, although I do like those two gifts a lot."

"How about the blue and black plaid flannel shirt I gave you? It'll be really warm on those cold winter mornings out at the job site."

"I'm trying to be serious here."

"Sorry. I don't have a clue what gift you're most thankful for this year."

"You're sure about that? Because recently I've tried to make it pretty clear how I feel about us."

"Yes, you have, but I'd love to hear you say it aloud just one more time," Amber teased with a flirtatious smile.

The couple stopped walking as Dallas took off to chase a squirrel. The two turned to face each other. "I'm thankful for the gift of your love, Amber. You've made such a positive difference in my life."

"I feel the same way about you." Then she stood on tiptoe and graced his lips with an affectionate kiss. "Does that convince you of my feelings for you?"

"Yep," Paul murmured before he leaned in for another taste of Amber's lips.

They stood in their embrace for several minutes until Dallas returned with a stick that he promptly dropped at his master's feet.

"You're so sly, Dallas. I'd never guess that *you* of all earthly creatures would want to play fetch." Turning toward Amber, he asked, "Do you mind if we play for a few minutes?"

She nodded in agreement, "Go ahead, boys."

Turning to Dallas, Paul said, "You win, Dallas. Fetch!" as he threw the stick high in the air. The dog took off after the flying stick and caught it in his mouth just before it touched the ground. Man's best friend and man played fetch for about a quarter of an hour while Amber looked on.

All at once Paul called Dallas to him. "Sit. Stay," he commanded firmly. Dallas obeyed instantly and waited at full alert for Paul's next command. Silently, Paul leaned over to pet Dallas briefly before feeding him a treat.

"What's going on?" Amber asked after waiting patiently for a couple of minutes. "Why did you stop playing fetch with Dallas?"

Paul turned and looked at Amber with an intensity she had never before observed in him. The longer he was silent, the more apprehensive she became.

"What's wrong?"

Dallas looked from man to woman and back to Paul as if he were trying to figure out what was going on between the couple. Unbelievably, Dallas remained firmly anchored in his sitting position. Paul handed Dallas another treat before moving closer to Amber.

"Nothing is wrong," Paul said, finally breaking the silence. "In fact, everything in my life is absolutely perfect, that is with the exception of one little thing."

Amber's raised eyebrows signaled that he had her undivided attention.

"I have one more gift for you." Kneeling down on a soft bed of pine needles, Paul looked up at his lovely lady and took her quivering hands in his. "Amber, I've come to love you deeply and cherish you over the past few weeks. You're everything and more than I've ever dreamed of finding in a woman. You're kind to the core, loving and compassionate toward me and others, and beautiful inside and out beyond compare."

Amber nodded slowly, bewilderment clouding her lovely face. Paul sensed that she still hadn't grasped what his stream of conversation was leading up to.

"Through prayer and reflection I've come to believe that you're a major part of God's plan for my life. I believe that you're the woman God intends to be my soul mate, best friend, life partner, and mother of our children."

Amber's dramatic intake of air alerted Paul that his one true love had finally realized what he was trying to communicate to her.

"Amber, will you make me the happiest man on earth and marry me? Soon? You can think about it if you want and let me know sometime in the *very* near future what your answer will be."

Falling to her knees Amber hugged him tightly and shouted with glee, "I don't need to think about my answer. Yes! Absolutely! I will marry you! Very soon!"

Paul reached into his coat pocket and unveiled a black velvet box tied with a bright, festive red ribbon. Amber untied the ribbon with trembling hands and was astounded when Paul opened the box to reveal a magnificent ruby and diamond engagement ring set in platinum.

She covered her mouth with her gloved hand as her eyes grew wide. "I'm speechless. Honestly, it's the most beautiful ring I've ever seen. Thank you so much."

"Here, try it on." He removed the ring from the box as Amber pulled off her left glove. As he slid the ring on her waiting finger, Paul said softly, "A perfect fit—just like you and I." Then he kissed her with all of the love in his heart, communicating a promise of all of the sweet tomorrows the couple had in store. As they continued their embrace, Paul gently caressed Amber's hair and cheek until she leaned away from him. The moment was magical for both of them.

"I love you so much, Paul. You've made me so happy this Christmas. I just know I'll be saying that same thing to you for the next fifty or sixty Christmases." Amber's eyes glistened with unshed tears.

As the couple stood and paused to admire Amber's newest gift, Paul rubbed his face, sighed deeply, and murmured, "Thank goodness that's over."

Placing her hands on her hips in a defensive stance, Amber said, "What is *that* supposed to mean?"

"That's supposed to mean that I haven't slept much for the past few nights for worrying that you would turn down my proposal."

"Faith, Paul. Faith in God's never-ending love and blessings."

He leaned closer and kissed his fiancée silent to prove that he did, in fact, have great faith in God's plan for their lives.

❄ ❄ ❄

After a few more heartfelt moments of sharing their hopes and dreams for their life together, Paul suggested they return to the house before darkness fell. "Even though I wouldn't mind spending more time with you, I'd hate to get lost out here in the woods without a flashlight or lantern."

The couple had begun walking back to the house arm in arm before Paul realized that Dallas wasn't at his side. "Come, Dallas." He leaned down to scratch Dallas's head just behind his ears, a favorite spot of the well-loved canine's. "You're a good old dog. Here's a little Christmas treat for your trouble, boy," and he pulled half a dozen small doggie treats from a bag in his pocket and fed them to his loyal pet. "Heel, Dallas." The trio began the trek back to Paul's house.

The bride-to-be babbled joyfully about Paul's

clever proposal and her engagement ring all the way back to the front yard. He gently tugged on her coat to get her to stop so they could talk before going inside to announce their engagement to their families. "When you accepted my proposal, you said you would marry me, and I quote, 'very soon.' Just how soon can I expect this wedding to take place, Miss Kellen?"

"How about Valentine's Day?" Amber answered without hesitating.

"Seriously? That's only six or seven weeks from today. Don't you women folk need a lot more time to plan a wedding than six or seven weeks?"

"Oh, honestly, Paul. I don't need any more time than that to prepare for our wedding. After all, I've been waiting my entire life for you to come along, my sweet groom." She tenderly touched his cheek and kissed him affectionately before turning toward home.

A Special Offer for My Readers

 *I*n chapter six of *A Holiday Miracle in Apple Blossom,* Mrs. Virginia Wrightmann created a very special handmade quilt especially for Mary Noel. To download your complimentary copy of the pattern and instructions for this delightful quilt, please visit my website at www.junemccraryjacobs.com. You can also follow me on my author's Facebook page to stay up to date with new blog posts and a free monthly sewing project.

I hope you enjoy creating this quilt for your own special angel as much as I enjoyed designing Mary Noel's quilt and creating the characters and plot for this debut novel.

With sincere appreciation,

June McCrary Jacobs

DISCUSSION
QUESTIONS

1. Compare and contrast the meanings of *compassion* and *kindness*. Is it possible to be compassionate without exhibiting kindness? Is it possible to be kind without feeling compassion?

2. Reflect on some occasions in your life when you were kind to another individual. How did that person react to your kindness? How did you feel about their reaction? How did your act of kindness make you feel about yourself?

3. Give some examples of occasions when you observed compassion in action. How did the act of compassion change the situation? How did compassion affect the individuals involved in the situation?

4. One of the characters in the book tells Paul that he and his wife are trying to encourage their sons to practice the "Golden Rule." How do you inspire the children and young people around you to practice the Golden

Rule daily in their own lives? Give some examples of how you practice this simple message in your own life.

5. Amber mentioned to Paul that she hadn't really made any friends since moving to Apple Blossom. What actions could Amber have taken to build some friendships even if the citizens of Apple Blossom didn't reach out to her first? Give an example of a time in your life when you reached out to someone in friendship. What happened as a result of your outreach?

6. Pastor Harris spent many hours visiting with and offering moral and spiritual support, comfort, and nurturing to Mary Noel's parents, Tim and Barbara Simmons. Have you ever felt comforted by the presence and words of a church or spiritual leader? How may you have felt if that individual had not intervened and ministered to you in your time of need?

7. Have you ever helped to organize a fund-raiser for a worthy cause? What was the reaction of those around you when you asked for their involvement and support in the event? What lesson can we learn from working together as a community to accomplish a common goal?

8. Mrs. Virginia Wrightmann carefully designed, embroidered and sewed together a unique patchwork quilt for Mary Noel. Has someone in your family or friendship circle ever made something especially for you? How did you feel upon receiving the gift? Have

you ever made a special gift or heirloom for someone you truly cared about? How did you feel upon giving the gift to the recipient?

9. Amber and Paul dated a relatively short time before his proposal, yet some couples date for a long time before discussing marriage. What guidelines do you believe couples should follow when determining if they will marry each other? What advice would you offer a young woman if she approached you with questions about this issue?

10. Amber and Paul will have a brief engagement before their wedding. Reflect upon the benefits and downfalls of a short engagement versus a long engagement. What considerations beyond convenience should the couple make when choosing their wedding date? Discuss the importance of both parties being in agreement on the length of their engagement and the date chosen for their wedding.